ARGON

E. L. PATRICK

Copyright © 2017 by E. L. Patrick

ISBN 978-0-9958141-0-3 (paperback)
ISBN 978-1-310-79409-4 (ebook)

Cover design by James T. Egan of Bookfly Design

Trade Paperback Edition

www.ELPatrick.com

to my parents,
for never quitting

ARGON

ONE

Life in Argon had been just about perfect before the slide ate Jimmy.

After three moves in two years, Robbie Larsen's first summer in his new town had been a hit. He'd met Jimmy Richmond on Day One, an instant friend with fierce loyalty and an open heart. Jimmy introduced him to Trent and the rest of the gang, who showed him what summer was all about. They spent most days biking, hiking, exploring . . . anything, as long as it was fun and they were together.

Trent and Jimmy knew all the best skateboard jumps, bike paths, and hideaways, like the short ridges that stretched along the bank of the mud-brown Red River, curling back on themselves and offering just enough space underneath for a boy. One tight squeeze to get under the lip and no one would be the wiser.

Jimmy stuck up for Robbie when the cute girls teased and took the blame when they got caught sneaking donuts from Mr. Grindelsson, a balding Swede whose bakery filled the nearby streets with the unmatchable odour of morning-fresh pastry. Weeks of friendship felt like years to Robbie—an unexpected bond that drew him to Jimmy as though they'd grown up together.

The summer of adventure gave way to autumn in Argon, and school. The bike rides grew shorter and the gang ended up most evenings at the school playground after supper. Robbie figured he was getting too old for playgrounds, but it was central and convenient for everyone to play out the string after the excitement of the day, especially when tasked with having to let little siblings tag along from time to time.

The boys enjoyed the playground more for the risks than anything: Who could climb the rock wall fastest and leap from the top the farthest? Who could swing the merry-go-round hardest or, for that matter, hang off backward longest without falling? And for late nights, who could bring the most smokes or cold ones from their father's collection without getting caught?

On this chilly Tuesday evening, the boys kept warm with a game of Twisties, a form of tag that only counted if you left a mark, and Robbie was It. Jimmy had been running along the swinging bridge on the playground, swaying as he made for the top of the big slide. Robbie knew he'd made contact with his desperation swipe as Jimmy scaled the ladder because Jimmy had cried out in pain and a little anger, even as he denied the tag and bounced across the bridge like a rabbit over hot coals.

Robbie was frustrated ("You're dead, Jimmy!"), but faked climbing up the rope ladder and jumped back down when Jimmy vanished into the tunnel that led to the slide's launch point. Robbie ran for the bottom of the slide, intending to trap his helpless prey as Jimmy slid. This tag would be undeniable.

But something beat him to it.

Robbie wasn't yet within arm's reach when the end of the slide sprung to life and curled in on itself like shaved wood. Robbie stopped short, shocked. The support pole bolted to the bottom popped up as the slide curled, flinging sand in a staccato burst from the quiet explosion. Then from inside the curl, Robbie saw what looked like a mouth begin to form. There was no fanfare as the hole opened; no roar, no sound. Only a silent, toothless yawn.

Jimmy didn't see it because he was making a face at Robbie as he slid into view from the tunnel. The others didn't see it because they were hiding. Robbie watched, horrified, feeling his eyes grow ever bigger, sure that they would soon pop out and roll from their sockets to the crystal sand below.

The hole was visible hardly more than a second. Jimmy, with a goofy look pasted on his face and—yes, there it was—a ragged scratch forking across his arm like lightning, stuck out his feet on instinct, anticipating touchdown. His feet never touched sand. He slid under the curl and into the hole without a sound, and the mouth clamped its invisible lips together and disappeared.

Jimmy was gone.

TWO

Robbie heard the front porch step squeak all the way from his upstairs bedroom.

His door was closed, but the sound slithered through his window like the worm wriggling in his conscience. His heart had long since slowed since his run from the playground, but now thumped loudly enough in his ears to keep him from hearing the conversation downstairs. The tone was clear, however, as was the visitor's shrill voice.

Jimmy's mom.

Sweat oozed from Robbie's neck as the talking stopped, replaced by the soft padding of his mother's footsteps on the stairs. There were thirteen steps—he had counted when they moved in, and hadn't liked that at all—and he felt the tiny vibrations from every one of them crawling through the carpet and under his door like those robotic killing machines in that PKD short he'd read.

Screamers, they called them. Or maybe that was in the movie version.

Mellie Larsen knocked and opened the door an inch. "Robbie?"

He didn't reply.

She pushed the door open wider and poked her head into his room. "Jimmy's mom says he didn't come home yet. Do you know where he is?"

He shook his head, afraid his voice might give him away. It wasn't a lie, exactly. He *didn't* know where Jimmy was.

"You were with him before supper, I thought."

He nodded, trying to look in her direction but avoiding her eyes. Trying to convince her (and maybe himself) that everything was all right as he decided how much to tell. He was certain of what he had seen, but he knew how unbelievable it would sound to his mom. She'd accused him of stretching the truth to stay out of trouble before—and of course he *had*—but this kind of story wouldn't even get him in the front door, as his dad would say.

Also, he wasn't stupid. He knew how many times his family had moved in the last two years, and how hard it was to settle. This was the first time in all that time that he'd found real friends. If he told the truth, they'd call him a liar for sure. There was no way any of them would believe *this*.

But what if he didn't tell and it happened again?

"This is important, Robbie. They're looking for him and your dad's going out to join them. Can you think of anything that might help them know where to look?"

Robbie cleared his throat and chewed his upper lip. If he told her a search was pointless he would need to explain why, but he couldn't. Oh, he could verbalize what he had seen, but that would unleash the cold terror that lurked among the words, like speaking a curse into existence.

And it would make him the laugh of the town. The stupid kid willing to say anything for attention.

"No." The word burned his throat like bile rising. A knot formed within him as he lied, but he couldn't risk telling. He couldn't bear having to move again.

He wanted to explain what happened, maybe *needed* to, but what good would telling do? Even if he hadn't imagined it, maybe the thing didn't kill Jimmy, just . . . took him. Swallowed him whole. He had disappeared to somewhere. Didn't that mean he might come back?

He managed to tell his mom that he would go with Dad and help with the search. It was the least he could do. *It's what Jimmy would do,* he thought as he slipped his jacket on and felt the knot in his belly begin to burn.

∞ ∞ ∞

The western sun was fading when Kevin Grinberg got the call from his brother-in-law, Terry. He couldn't understand him at first through the shrieks in the background—Kevin's sister, Veronica, crying and barking desperate orders while the men spoke—but the news broke through.

Jimmy hadn't come home.

Terry had already crisscrossed Argon once in less than twenty minutes and was gathering anyone available at the small water treatment plant by the river. When Kevin arrived, two dozen men had formed pairs and trios to comb the river's edge and each street running west to east on the town grid.

Kevin walked east with his friend, Thomas Larsen, and their sons. Trent wouldn't let his father out of the house alone that night, so Kevin told him to wear a jacket and bring his flashlight. Trent and Jimmy had been inseparable since childhood, and Robbie had fit in like another cousin since his family arrived in June. Kevin knew his son wouldn't sleep until the search was over, and suspected the same of Robbie.

The foursome bathed the ditches and trees with light as they made their way along the street; the adults on one side, the boys on the other. Between them rode Walt Blackwell (an aging mechanic who owned the town's only gas station), who kept his windows down and his high beams up, the soft growl of the engine the only noise among them as they inched along.

Walt wasn't Kevin's first choice of partners for any endeavour, let alone a tour through town together, but Terry had grouped them by default on account of Kevin having married Walt's daughter, Susanna. *The things you do for love,* Kevin had reminded himself many times in the years since their wedding, whenever contact with Walt was necessary.

That was often, unfortunately. Apart from meeting the expectation of family loyalty in a small town, Kevin had (somehow!) allowed his father-in-law to fund his motel operation next to Walt's Wrench & Gas. Kevin managed the Country Rose Cafe and Restaurant in Argon ("Free Refills!" the large sign said just beneath the painted rose, though it didn't specify free refills of *what,* opening the door for the odd smart aleck to request free seconds of food rather than coffee) and didn't dare let Walt into that enterprise. The motel was a side project to revive the old lot next to Walt's station that Susanna had thought would be a good family venture. Kevin loved her, but what he thought of her business sense he kept to himself.

He also kept quiet his knowledge that Walt had injected himself surreptitiously into at least a half dozen other businesses thanks to his generous desire to own the whole town. He didn't know for *certain* that they all weren't fair business dealings, but he did know that at least two of the "partners" had felt cornered into agreements and he had seen for himself that Walt treated partnerships like dictatorships.

ARGON

(It was a wonder Susanna's parents were still together.)

But Walt was family. Or, at the very least, his wife was, and he didn't want to jeopardize her relationship with Walt or himself. That, and he wasn't convinced enough people would have the guts to climb out from under Walt's thumb for such a revelation to make any difference.

They sighted no movement from west to east, and rumbled north the few blocks in Walt's truck as per Terry's instructions: walk to the end of the street, drive to the edge of town, work your way south.

∞ ∞ ∞

"Why'd you take off like that?"

The adults were inside the cab, but even alone in the back of Walt's pickup with nothing but the whistling breeze, Trent spoke to Robbie with a deliberate hush.

Robbie tensed as the slide returned to his mind's eye, curling over itself like a toboggan or a fish hook just before it took Jimmy. Yes, very much like a fish hook, and Jimmy was the fish now, flopping and gasping for air somewhere on the bottom of some sinister boat after having been reeled in by . . . by what, exactly? He'd heard stories of girls and boys being snatched in the bigger cities he'd lived in, but hadn't thought it could happen here. And this was no white van with tinted windows that was responsible, though this was no less sinister.

"Had to get home. Almost bedtime. Bec and I had to get home."

"You were biking pretty hard. You didn't even finish the game." Trent's voice turned quizzical and strained. "And Jimmy took off, too. Left his bike, too. At first I thought you guys were mad or something. Now the whole town's lookin' for him." He slammed an open palm on the rippled truck bed. "Robbie . . ."

His voice cracked like eggshell as he posed the question Robbie had already asked himself a hundred times:

"What if we can't find him?"

∞ ∞ ∞

"Pay 'tention to those bushes, boys!" Walt Blackwell's harsh voice cut across Robbie and Trent in perfect unison with the beam of his flashlight. "He won't be jumpin' out atcha, you've gotta *look*."

Blackwell watched them stiffen and smiled to himself as they batted the bushes along the road with renewed vigour. *Crank up the alert level, boys. This is men's work.* He didn't suffer passengers in general and didn't much like the Larsen kid, what with his daddy's attitude and all. If Trent got caught up in some verbal crossfire, so be it. Might toughen him up some.

Blackwell hadn't liked Thomas Larsen since Day One. Since *before* Day One, as a matter of fact. Last winter, Larsen had contacted him about renting the grand turn-of-the-century home of Stella Regent Blackwell listed for sale online. Blackwell was adamant that the house was for sale, not rent. Renters were transient creatures, which didn't behoove Walt Blackwell one bit. Besides, referring another mortgage to Stanley Gnocci at the red brick Bank of Nova Scotia on Main would mark his name a little darker in Stanley's good books. And as a businessman, Walt knew that Stanley's books were the gold standard in this town.

But Larsen had been the most serious caller in months and Blackwell wasn't about to waste the opportunity. The house had belonged to Blackwell's mother, and after some early interest following her funeral a year before, the well had run dry and he was tiring of the burden of upkeep inherited with the home.

Armed with that information, Larsen leveraged his way into a rental agreement. Blackwell knew when he was cornered, but he was also a sour loser who harboured no illusion of taking the high road. He filed away Larsen's peculiarities for future use, like avoiding a mortgage and refusing a yearly rental agreement (much to Blackwell's embarrassment, the newcomer wrestled him into accepting a simple damage deposit plus monthly advance payments). If Blackwell were the type, he might have wondered why this fellow had such an aversion to setting down roots. Or thought aloud the same in the presence of witnesses.

He became further irritated when his grandkids, Trent and Roseli, took to Larsen's own kids over the summer, and told them as much. Told them Larsen was a mean man, and you don't associate with meanies or their families. Not that they listened to a word he said; twelve and six with not a care in the world.

Fool kids.

Blackwell looked down the charcoal nose of his brand-spankin'-new F-150 and scowled at Trent and the Larsen kid, Robbie. They had wandered again from the side of the road and were walking ten feet in front of the truck. Trent aimed his flashlight into the ditch, but the Larsen kid pointed his straight down the road into his own shadow while his left hand dangled at his side.

Idiot.

Blackwell poked his head out the window again and yelled them back to roadside. As they slowed, he caught a glimpse of Robbie's fingertips in the Ford's beam and something dark, like ink or mud, smeared across the middle three on his left hand. Or—Blackwell sighed—blood, from swatting the bushes.

He slid the gear from D to P and stepped out onto the road. "Hold up, kid, you're bleeding." He called Larsen over, while the idiot kid just stood staring at his fingers like they were worms crawling out from the end of his palms. As Blackwell drew up beside the boy, the fingertips shone, bright and colourless, in the light converging from their two flashlights. Tiny black clumps of dirt clung to the underside of Robbie's fingernails like barnacles to a schooner. In the bright white of the Maglites, Blackwell could see the small streaks of blood that must have rolled from Robbie's fingertips down to the ridge under his nails. Blackwell frowned. They hadn't been out here long, but the blood didn't look fresh.

Then he was inches away and could see that the dirt wasn't dirt. His hackles raised as a chill slithered up his back like a silent finger tracing its way from his thick waistline to his wide collar. He brought the light within three inches of Robbie's fingers to confirm his suspicion. No, that wasn't dirt at all. It looked like . . .

Flesh.

∞ ∞ ∞

"What's that?"

Robbie jumped as Trent's grandpa barked at him and jabbed the flashlight beam at his eyes. He'd been staring at his fingers since "Old Walt" (as most kids snorted when he wasn't in range) stopped the truck and told him he was bleeding. He'd been puzzled for only the time it took to raise his hand into the light, before remembering his final tag on the playground; the one Jimmy had felt but ignored as he raced across the swinging bridge to his doom. The scene looped over in front of Robbie as if projected onto his hand while he gawked at his blood-stained fingers. How had he not noticed the blood when it was fresh, when he ran home from the playground?

Then Old Walt's flashlight was blinding him, and he didn't know how to answer the question. The simple question with the "you'd better have a good explanation for this" tone.

He *did* have a good explanation for his bloody fingers, but all Robbie thought as he looked at his hand was that connecting those dots to his missing friend was not a good idea right now. Telling the truth could lead to the *whole* truth, and Robbie didn't think the whole truth would qualify as a good explanation to Old Walt. He stared at the man, feeling time stretch slowly with every drum beat of his heart, not knowing what to say. He couldn't think clearly enough even to formulate a lie—his mind was stuck on the projector loop of clawing red lightning across Jimmy's birch-white arm, seeing Jimmy's goofy smile, watching Jimmy vanish into the end of the slide—so he opened his mouth to hear what he'd say.

"N-nothing."

The flashlight dipped down just enough for Robbie to see Old Walt blink, like a crocodile contemplating its prey. Before the death roll.

Then Robbie's father was there, pushing the light away from his eyes and wiping his fingers, guiding him through the darkness, away from Old Walt and Trent and Mr. Grinberg. Toward home, to wash him up and make sure—for at least this moment—that everything was all right.

∞ ∞ ∞

With Thomas and Robbie gone, the remaining trio formed a human triangle in Blackwell's pickup—Kevin up front with his father-in-law, Trent in the bed of the truck—and drove ahead at a walker's pace. All three fired bolts of daylight from their Maglites into the bushes.

Blackwell mashed his lips together in a concentrated pucker. "You get a look at the kid's hands?"

"Robbie's? No, why?"

Blackwell glanced at Kevin's side of the cab. "Bloody as all hell." He knew he was exaggerating, but he had a point to make. "I'd bet Vegas that the crud under his nails was young Jimmy's skin. Which part, I dunno."

"What?" Kevin sounded like he had just been told his hair was on fire. "Are you crazy?"

"Shoulda seen it, Kev. He was scared shitless when I asked him what happened. Just stared at his fingers like a loon." No, he could do better than that. "Like a bug-eyed killer with his hand in the cookie jar."

"Walt, you *cannot* believe that! Robbie's a kid. Twelve, or eleven at least. Why would he—" Kevin shoulder-checked to make sure the sliding rear window was closed. He was pretty sure Trent (with the wind in his ears) wouldn't hear them through the lowered side windows, but the rear . . .

The rear window was latched up tight, but Kevin lowered his voice anyway. "Why would he kill Jimmy?"

"You read the papers. Why do any of those psychos kill? We dunno, but this kid ain't *from* here, Kev, and he tore *somethin'* up pretty damn good." Blackwell looked out through his window, as if addressing the darkness itself. "The killers are gettin' younger every time. They kill for sport. They kill because they can." He shook his head. "You know how messed the cities are these days. You used to live there."

Kevin scoffed. He didn't disagree with Walt's last sentiment, but he couldn't let his father-in-law get carried away. Robbie was *twelve*, and Kevin had seen for himself last summer how good a kid he was. "You need to get rid of that thinking, Walt. Right now. You accuse him of murder because of a . . . a bloody finger, and you'll lose credibility with a lot of this town."

Blackwell's eyelids lowered to half-mast as he tilted his head to face his son-in-law. Kevin had seen that squint before, and the older man's darkening face told him that Walt had no intention of listening to his advice. In fact, he was probably deciding to take Kevin's advice as an outright challenge.

"You seen anyone new at the mo-tel lately? Passing through?"

Kevin shook his head. "Motel's been dry since mid-August. That's typical." Business had been better back when the Canada-U.S. border crossing closed at night and poor planners had no place else to go. Now the odd dreg graced the dusty sheets while Kevin stood guard at the counter. "How about at the pumps?"

"Not a one. Not for a month, almost. Pumps have always been cheaper across the way, but with the dollar down, even the locals are driving by. Buncha ungrateful dickweeds." Walt stopped short of thanking Kevin for his two-fill-a-week habit. Family oughta be the first in line, he figured, and false praise was a waste of time.

They passed Morris Street and two houses in silence.

"No, we don't get much in the way o' new folks, Kevin. You know that." Blackwell set his flashlight on his lap and blew into his curled free hand. "You've gotten cozy with Larsen. If not his boy, what about him?"

"Thomas? C'mon, Walt, I know you don't like him, but he's a good guy."

"Could be both of 'em. Larsen rushed him off pretty quick. Maybe just did a better job of washing his own hands."

Kevin's eyes narrowed. "You're reaching."

"Y'know he's bounced around a bit the last while, I heard."

"Yeah, he told me. Couple jobs didn't work out, from what he says."

"What he says." The flashlight jiggled as Blackwell scooped it from his lap. "The man looks fine, Kevin. Jus' fine."

"Does he."

"So what, you suppose, is causin' a fine man—who looks employable and not at all suspicious—to drag his family from town to town, even change countries?"

"Could be anything, Walt."

"Ever wonder why he can't hold down a job?"

"Hadn't." He repeated himself to highlight the lunacy of Walt's implication. "Could be *anything*."

Blackwell peered down the barrel of his flashlight into the night. "Might be worthwhile to wonder."

Kevin stared at Blackwell, who did not return his gaze. The older man kept driving, waving his light across the street, the ditch, the bushes as others in the distance called out Jimmy's name.

THREE

Wednesday morning came too soon for Thomas Larsen. After getting Robbie to bed Tuesday evening, he'd spent three hours traipsing down Crow Wing Trail with Kevin Grinberg and a pair of halogens—a trip both tiring and spooky.

He'd walked the trail once in broken daylight, on a family hike in July as they ventured through their new surroundings (Bec had attracted a late season wood tick), but darkness had a way of breathing life into otherwise still surroundings. Thomas could handle the dark, but walking an old Indian trail to find a missing boy after midnight was bad for the imagination.

What kept him most from a peaceful sleep, though, was Robbie's reaction after coming home from the in-town search. Robbie had clammed right up after Walt's outburst, full of a lot of "nothing" on the walk home when Thomas asked what was going on. He wanted to believe Robbie, but Blackwell's reptilian stare irked Thomas on a good day—even more when it was being levelled at his son.

If it *was* something, Robbie would tell him. Always had, given time. Robbie was a good boy, if a little withdrawn. Oh, he could make friends, and had in all of their recent stops as far as Thomas knew, but Robbie had been growing quieter in recent months (or had it been longer?). Thomas reminded himself often, amid frustration, that he hadn't volunteered much to his own mother, either, when he'd been approaching teenhood. Would he have if his dad had been around?

And it wasn't Robbie's fault that he'd been dragged through three states—and now two countries—in so short a time. Thomas couldn't blame him for being upset—*he* didn't like it himself (he'd known military kids that didn't move that much) and the moves had been his decision.

Not that he felt he'd had much choice. Some things were best left behind.

Now, in Argon—the tiny town in a new land where everything had to work out—a child had vanished and Thomas didn't like what was brewing in Walt Blackwell's eyes: suspicion. Perhaps the past had simply made him paranoid. But Robbie couldn't be responsible for what had happened; Thomas hadn't seen as much as a trace in Robbie's twelve years that would point in that direction. It was unthinkable.

No, Blackwell had had it in for him since the beginning, since Blackwell had slipped up and Thomas pitched hardball for the rental agreement. He hadn't thought it would be an issue (it was just negotiation, after all) but Blackwell turned out to be real small town with real big pride.

Thomas had hoped his growing friendship with Blackwell's son-in-law would give him an in to smoothing the wrinkles from their original encounter, but that was before he learned that Kevin didn't much care for the older man either. Couldn't blame him.

Maybe Blackwell wasn't worth the effort. Maybe—despite Thomas's attempts to build bridges with everyone in Argon—

ARGON

Blackwell was so steeped in his ways that nothing would change his mind. Thomas had seen versions of this before—different towns, different times—but maybe people were just people, no matter where you moved.

But Blackwell or no, this was probably his last chance to make it work. Even though Mellie had been with him all the way (so far) on his crazy trek through four shrinking towns in two years, he'd noticed more frequently the barely-there tension in her jaw or the weary flicker in her eyes that preceded her support. But Argon was *it*. He'd been searching for a small, quiet town—a *community*—where he could finally settle his family in peace, and he'd found it. Their new home. Their last stop. Their final resting place, so to speak.

He didn't need to make it work with Blackwell, he reasoned to himself. Just be civil and expect nothing in return. Teach the kids that one bad apple doesn't have to spoil the lot. Everyone had to learn that eventually, but the sooner the better for Robbie and Bec. Shouldn't be too bad, he mused.

But for those crocodile eyes . . .

∞ ∞ ∞

By the time the Search and Rescue team rolled in from Highway 75 Wednesday after lunch, twenty hours had passed since Jimmy Richmond disappeared and Blackwell had spent two of them over morning coffee mulling over the likeliest locations Thomas Larsen could have disposed of the body.

The Red was atop the list—its muddy brown current probably no stranger to riverbed bodies along its hundred and fifty Canadian miles (two hundred and fifty *kilometers,* to be sure, but Blackwell had been around before metrication and hoped to live long enough to watch it die)—and he wouldn't bet a pound of roses on his dead mother's grave the search team would find anything anywhere but the river. Everyone knew missing kids didn't get found much after the first twenty-four hours—a deadline that was fast approaching despite the efforts that had carried on that morning.

He knew that Kevin had stayed out late and gotten up early to help the search for Jimmy, since Susanna was minding the orders in the Country Rose kitchen and had told him as much. After last night's search parties dwindled, Kevin and Larsen reloaded their Maglites and walked Crow Wing Trail through the forest to old Fort Dufferin, even though others had already checked that route.

Fort Dufferin stood—leaned, mostly—a couple of miles north of town on the west side of the river. The fort had been a key police post during Canada's infancy, but had been deserted since the 1880s and spent most of its summers as a spooky playground for kids and an occasional hideout for international fugitives. Double-checking its dozen old buildings was not a bad idea, but Blackwell liked to think maybe Kevin *had* paid attention last night and started wondering, too, if little Jimmy wasn't just lost, but taken.

Taken came up with the regular old timers coffee crew at the Country Rose, too, without any help from Blackwell. He was a decade or two away from full membership in that club, but had learned long ago that sitting one table over with his own cup of black-no-sugar kept his finger to the pulsing vein on the neck of the town. The old timers had theories for every day of the week but, more importantly, they also had sources.

On this morning, Blackwell learned that the RCMP had denied Mayor Wight's request for an Amber Alert, citing no concrete evidence of abduction. To Wight's credit, he'd thrown a fit over the phone until he'd at least earned the promise of an RCMP search team "on the ground by breakfast!" To the province's credit, they actually sent the Mounties the same day, a team of eight which was now drawing a large crowd at the Argon Fire Hall (tucked between the tiny Country Rose and the stately red brick Town Hall).

Blackwell would never claim to be a scholar, but he recognized an opportunity when he saw one. He had been considering an election run since Wight raised concerns over price gouging at Walt's Wrench & Gas last spring, and contributing to the search and rescue effort couldn't hurt. Especially if in the process he could show Wight for the incompetent sonuvabum he was. As a bonus, before long (if he was right about the kid and his father, that is) Thomas Larsen would be the most reviled man in town.

Rental agreement be damned.

∞ ∞ ∞

The RCMP search team set up base in the fire hall, which made sense for several reasons: the hall was central yet close to river access (one block north of Argon's busiest intersection of Main and Morris and a short roll from there over the west dike road), it held all of Argon's emergency plans, and it was usually—though certainly not today—vacant.

Argon's volunteer fire department had one part-time employee, custodian Lyle "Ripples" Maclean (so called because of the time when he'd been fishing the Red off the dock with friends as a youth and had fallen into the dirty, dark water with naught but a single splash; as big Donny Fricks told the story, he turned at the sound and saw nothing but ripples, so he reached through the ripples and found Lyle by the grace of God and a tee shirt collar, and hauled him up to the dock to claim the biggest catch of that day). Seventeen volunteer firefighters comprised the crew, including four women, which hadn't been news for years but still wagged tongues with the old timers coffee crew when they ran out of other topics to discuss.

The commotion outside the fire hall began with mostly retirees—those blessed with copious amounts of time and curiosity—milling about the large parking pad that paved the way from Church Street to the large brown doors of the fire hall (dark brown being the height of splendour on the building, which was coated mostly with a standard beige that had likely been cheaper than red at the time of council approval). Ripples—who'd jumped off the pot to start looking busy when he heard the trucks arrive—beamed when the mayor collared him to help with crowd control.

The crowd grew like a snowball sparking a slow avalanche as passersby paused en route to the Bigway with grocery list in hand or the post office with a real live letter. (The internet had killed much personal mail in Argon, as elsewhere, but not all of it yet.) The noseys ignored Ripples' pleas to "Keep yer distance!" as they inspected the police box trucks and chattered, waiting for someone to emerge from the fire hall.

Blackwell had walked the few steps from the Country Rose to rub a few shoulders. The growing buzz had become almost tangible. His friends and neighbours were no country hicks (not most, anyway), but flame attracted even the least curious moths. This was a sad event, but any event in Argon generated a crowd.

He caught pieces of theories and conversations as he elbowed his way toward the front of the pack:

black bear . . .

cougar . . .

taken . . . (there it was again, courtesy of one of the old timers)

best to go home and lock the doors

ARGON

Mayor Wight emerged from the fire hall with two strangers trailing. Once Ripples whistled the crowd into silence, Wight introduced the strangers as Arlene Salomann, search team lead, and Connor Tymchuk, dive crew chief. The crowd murmured loudly—including one audible moan—at the phrase *dive crew,* as though Wight had called Tymchuk the chief of No Hope Remains.

Blackwell exchanged glances with Wes Slater—as tall as he was lean—towering over Blackwell's left shoulder. Slater was a regular at Walt's Wrench & Gas, one of the good ones that held loyalty in higher regard than the siren call of cheap American fuel. (Plus, he brought more beer than he drank to Friday poker nights and Blackwell liked that in a man.) Slater nodded, as though given permission to unlock his tongue and spill his mind. He turned back to face Wight as the murmuring subsided. "Ya gonna drag the river? If someone took him, the kid won't be in the Red!"

"Oh, geez!" Wight hissed with a venomous mix of anger and fear. "Wes, don't be stupid. Jimmy's lost, not kidnapped. You're only going to scare folks!"

"If he's lost, why'djou call in a dive team so soon?" Several shouts echoed around Slater, spurring him on with that special confidence birthed by public approval. "He didn't come home after school so you think he's in the river. Why the leap?"

Wight glared at him. "I didn't call in a *dive team,* Wes. I called for a search team and they sent divers, too. They're here, so we're going to let them do their job. It won't hurt. You were out there last night, Wes. We searched. If Jimmy was in town we would've found him. Kevin and Terry even tried ag—"

Blackwell cut him off with a scowl. "What if he went south?"

Argon was a border town on the north side of the 49th parallel, unique in that it rubbed up against two states and, not long before, two border crossings. The Minnesota port of entry and its dependent community had withered and eventually closed after North Dakota's crossing two miles over upgraded in the wake of 9/11. Even with the former passage lined with concrete traffic barricades, it wouldn't take much for a theoretical kidnapper to cross with his quarry on foot to a waiting vehicle stashed in the tiny American ghost town next door. The town's south dike would even help provide cover.

"Brought state troopers on both sides up to speed last night and sent pictures, so they're keeping eyes out. We'll keep fanning out from town as long as people are able to search, and hope to high heaven the divers find nothing the whole time."

Slater scoffed. "As long as they keep finding nothin', I say lock the kids inside. Damn right it'll scare folks, but they're scared anyway."

"Wes, you're not helping. School stays open. We're going to keep that going for the kids' sake, and every adult who can shut up shop awhile can join the search or get out of the way."

Blackwell wouldn't deny that routine was important, especially for the kids (he'd probably make the same decision as mayor), but consensus would do nothing to set him up for next fall's election. "I dunno, Wilf. Seems pretty careless to let the kids roam around before we sort this out."

"They won't be *roa*—" Wight stopped and blew an angry breath. "Stop wasting time. If we find a need to cancel school for a while, we'll do it. For now, I'm turning things over to the search team. Best we can do right now is follow their lead."

A smirk tugged at the corners of Blackwell's eyes, but he carved a wooden face as he lowered his voice (though not low enough for Wight to miss the parting shot). "If the kids roam free and this happens again, it's on your head, Wilf." He shook his head as Arlene

ARGON

Salomann stepped forward to address the crowd. "It's on your head."

∞ ∞ ∞

By two o'clock on Wednesday afternoon, the search team had mobilized nearly one hundred of the town's able-bodied to walk the streets and scour the riverbanks (this time with trained dogs) and expand the human net beyond town to the expansive farmland surrounding Argon. Three dogs joined the searchers in the fields, with two aerial drones providing a birds-eye view and sending images to base. The dive team consisted of six Mounties, aided by Donny Fricks's dad, Don Senior, who'd done some dives during his time with the Ontario Provincial Police and even one in Argon when the Prokowski kid drove home drunk from the States on the frozen Red River.

The kid had been drinking till closing time on the North Dakota side and picked the cleverest way he could think up to skip the border crossing and the DUI charge that would surely find him there. Almost made it, too. He actually overshot the boat launch ramp and passed under the old green bridge connecting Argon to Highway 75 before realizing his mistake. He was turning around when the ice gave way and swallowed his white Ford whole. Fortunately for Prokowski, he had bragged about the plan to his buddies at the bar and they were waiting at the launch ramp when he went under. In the still air of that cold November night, one of them would later say, the cracking ice sounded like a small forest giving way to a single swipe from the mighty hand of God; the bright eyes of the truck rolled from their straightforward stare to petition the heavens for an awkward moment before the river reached up to suck the sticks of light into its swirling darkness.

When the shock wore off for the witnesses (as much as there was to witness in the middle of night), one of them raced to the police station a few blocks west of the river and called for help. Fricks soon received the call to dust off his old diving suit and lead the local officers in the diving effort. He did so without hesitation and ended up making the rescue before the frightened young drunk took in too much water (probably because he was too full of booze to make room for anything more), but later said it was the darkest and eeriest dive he'd ever experienced, being used to the blue waters of southern Ontario.

That had been years ago, and Blackwell knew that Fricks considered the Prokowski incident his last rescue dive. He'd heard Fricks say so several times over coffee at the Country Rose. The water had a way of telling a diver when it was time to go, Fricks would say, and the mud dark Red—ice cold with zero visibility, what divers called black water—had given him a clear sign that night. (Beyond that, Fricks was vague, but Blackwell got the sense the dive had reminded Fricks of his mortality or some such bull, which would explain him taking up the cloth and parking at First Baptist.) Besides, who was Fricks kidding? His old dry suit had been a tight squeeze back *then,* and the man hadn't gotten any trimmer.

But Fricks still knew enough to be Wight's town lead for the dive crew, and Blackwell was a firm believer in that old adage about the company you keep. Credibility came from the shoulders you rubbed more than the hands you helped. As long as the search was on, it was time to stick to Fricks.

Blackwell broke off from his assigned search crew in town after twenty minutes to double back to the shop and hit a washroom (and make sure Sam, his mechanic, wasn't in over his head with the day's appointments), then drove across the old green bridge and down to the boat ramp on the west side of the river. The river was where the action was, and he couldn't go long without being in the know—one of his strengths, he always figured; people needed men who would take what they knew and lead, not just figureheads like Wight who deferred responsibility because they were too afraid to make real decisions.

True to form, Wight stood on the dock and watched as Fricks did most of the talking with Connor Tymchuk, the dive crew chief. The dive team had set up their trucks at the top of the boat ramp and a single boat was holding steady about fifty yards downstream, halfway between the dock and the bridge. Blackwell could see one man in the boat, no doubt checking the on-board computer for signs of activity while the rest of the crew fished around below.

Blackwell made no effort to step gingerly as he left the gravel path for the wood-slat dock, and the other men turned to face him when the dock sloshed under the added weight. "Find anything?"

"Whole lotta nothing," Wight replied, running fingers through his thinning hair.

The crew chief agreed. "The Red's a wet junkyard. Sonar reads a lot of noise but it's mostly garbage and holes. Be thankful this isn't your drinking water." He chuckled. "I recommend you keep funding your treatment plant if you don't want an outbreak of something nasty."

"Holes?"

Fricks gave him a nod. "Small disturbances, pockets of movement that disappear before the divers get there. Or never *were* there. Could be undertow, could be fish." He grunted. "Red herrings." He smiled grimly at the unintended pun then shook his head. "This will take a while."

"Ever think of starting further downstream?" Blackwell asked. "By the homes?"

Wight's hair danced as he nodded his head vigorously, and Blackwell thought the mayor's hair might slide off his head entirely. "They're already downstream. The second crew went up past River Road and 200 to work back from there." Wight frowned. "But what *about* the homes?"

Blackwell shrugged. "Just thinkin'. We've covered a good lotta ground since last night with no luck. The kid's got no reason to run away, and he ain't three or four. He'd know better than to get close to the water when he's alone. Maybe this was no accident."

Wight's greying eyebrows reached for his receding hairline and missed by a country mile. "Walt! We can't be pushing that crazy idea right now. Too many parents are gonna be thinking that already, so we can't let them play into it."

Wight glanced at the other men for support. Fricks pursed his lips in thought while Tymchuk stared out over the river and took a long drag of crisp October air. The dive chief pulled his gaze from the river to face Walt. "Always a consideration. We can't ignore the idea, but what kind of evidence you have to go with that thinking?"

The Larsen boy's flesh-stained fingers splayed in Blackwell's mind like a disembodied hand against the glass wall of his skull, pressing to break free. Was it evidence? *He* thought so, but he also knew his current company. Wight didn't like him much and Fricks was a man of calm and control. Neither were likely to back him on this without absolute proof, but he didn't need them on board yet. Just needed to open them up to the possibility, and maybe the old timers and their theories could take it from there. If not, he knew plenty more people who liked to listen and he had plenty more talk to send their way. "Like I said, just thinkin'. Can't close our minds to the options, no matter how much we don't like 'em."

Wight shook his head, looking troubled. "I really can't see it. I did raise that angle to get the search team here faster,"—Wight looked almost sheepish as he glanced at Tymchuk—"but I can't honestly imagine anyone would be interested in taking a twelve-year-old boy. Not here."

Blackwell wanted to smack him for his irritating naïveté but kept his voice level. If Wight was going to figure this out, he'd have to take the slow road. "The second-busiest border crossing from coast to coast is a two-minute drive from where we're standing, Wilf. Who knows what kind of crazies drive past town every day? Not to mention we got new folks in town who we really don't know much about yet. We can't just *not imagine* it away." Blackwell raised both hands palms out, as if begging forgiveness. "Look, I'd rather put the idea t'rest too, and frankly, you're right. We don't need people talkin' that way. I say we keep that thinkin' to ourselves and hope we don't ever have to open that door." He shrugged. "But we can't ignore it as an option if we're gonna do right by this boy."

Wight nodded in a way that made Blackwell think he was just buying time. He could see the mayor didn't want him there. Clear thinking made the man uncomfortable. He was a decent mayor for a quiet town, but Blackwell supposed Argon wouldn't be so quiet much longer. Not if he had anything to say about it.

He knew everything the trio standing with him on the dock had to say: *whole lotta nothing*. The river was long and the current was strong, which made it the best place in Argon to dump a body. The dive team was only getting started, but the likelihood of finding the boy in this dark soup grew more bleak with every passing hour. Blackwell's chest burned with a sense of justice as he cursed Larsen silently. Larsen couldn't get away with this, not on his watch. If there was no evidence to be found (young Robbie's fingers rose again in his mind with a menacing wave), he would have to make sure that didn't matter.

The Country Rose would be the perfect place to start. Once the old timers coffee crew got wind of the right details—not the whole story (since he didn't have that) but just enough to drive the bus— word would spread across town like a killing virus through an unsuspecting bloodstream. "Or a vaccine through an *infected* one," he muttered to himself. Yes, that was it. People needed the info so they could make the best decision. The right decision.

He would have to take what he knew and *lead*.

FOUR

Morning recess had terrified Robbie. He'd wanted so much to tell the teachers about the slide and keep the kids away from the ... whatever it was that had taken Jimmy last night, but then he got to thinking about the chain of events that would follow.

Extrapolation, as Mrs. Schultz would say in afternoon Math. Robbie didn't like extrapolation, because it seemed to be just another doorway to *fear.* Fear of what would come. Fear of the future. And mixed in with that action-freezing fear, another fear that his hesitation was the wrong choice, that he was endangering others by waiting.

But he didn't say a word. As he sat under the large willow in the schoolyard, keeping a watchful eye on the kids around the slide, all of the tell-the-truth futures Robbie envisioned took him away from Argon. He couldn't allow that. He couldn't convince himself—not in the space of morning recess—that life without Argon would be his best option. Despite Jimmy's disappearance, Robbie still had great friends here that had proved themselves in four short months. That hadn't happened elsewhere since ... forever.

Then recess was over. Every child staggered back to class, wishing the rest of the morning away so they could get back to playtime. And Robbie had never been so relieved.

Nothing had happened.

Wednesday's lunch hour had been only slightly less terrifying. Robbie sat under the willow again, hardly touching his food, watching the slide and replaying Jimmy's last moments, breaking them down step-by-step like an investigator at a crime scene:

They'd been running.

They'd been playing Twisties, running around the sandlot that surrounded the playground.

Trent had tagged him, so he was chasing Jimmy, who wasn't the slowest of the gang but was closest. He'd chased Jimmy past the gym rings and circled the swing set. Then Jimmy had crossed the swinging bridge to the slide when he decided to head for—no, wait. He had *tagged* Jimmy by the rings and Jimmy ignored it. He had yelled at Jimmy as he circled the swing set. Something angry.

You're dead, Jimmy!

You're dead, Jimmy.

And moments later, it had come true. His *curse* had come true. Because that's what it was, right? Some kind of curse. An unintentional prediction that one of his best friends was about to die.

The thought summoned tears that he blinked away in the shade of the willow. He wanted to turtle—just tuck his head between his knees right there in the schoolyard and rock until Mom came to find him. But he wasn't a kid anymore. He wouldn't let anyone see him cry. *Why are you crying* was an embarrassing question on its own, but Robbie didn't like the questions that would follow as he extrapolated yet again. Nobody needed to know that Jimmy's death was his fault. Confessing wouldn't change a thing. And now that he knew what had happened, he would just make sure not to threaten anyone, even for fun.

Maybe that's why Dad had always said that words are as dangerous as rocks if you throw them at people.

Then Maddy squealed from a playground swing, and Robbie snapped his head up. Bec's friend, Maddy—little, annoying, always controlling Maddy—rode the center swing on her knees, gripping the chains as she vaulted back and forth with her ponytail flapping behind her like a dead carp dangling. No trouble, just . . . Maddy. Robbie turned up his nose and watched her fly for a few moments before a terrible thought wormed into his mind.

What if he could do it again?

If he could snatch her little, annoying, always controlling face from the seat of the swing—if he could *control* the hole that had eaten Jimmy—then he wouldn't have to worry about it happening again. If he could start it, he could stop it. And eventually (*maybe*) he could even figure out what happened to Jimmy and bring him back home.

Robbie eyed Bec's friend from his lonely seat under the willow tree. The rest of the schoolyard disappeared slowly, fading out of focus until he could see only Maddy—framed by the willow's dying tendrils that hung just inside his periphery—swinging from her knees and mouthing silent squeals. The swing seemed to slow to match the rhythm of his heart: back and forth, back and forth. For a moment, Robbie only watched. Then his lips smacked as he pulled them apart just enough to whisper, "You're dead, Maddy."

"You're dead, Maddy."

"You're dead, Maddy."

The sandlot sang with the cries of happy children, but Robbie heard nothing as he scanned the playground. Daredevils both large and small scaled the eight-foot climbing wall with only a prayer between them and the packed sand below. The swinging bridge shook as Grade Two boys played Pirates and fought for control of the gang-plank. The seesaw pistoned up and down like a pumpjack smelling oil. The slide looked calm and inviting—certainly not hungry enough to snatch another unsuspecting child. The swings . . . (Robbie's heart beat faster as he waited for the hole to appear behind Maddy to swallow her up and take her away. His mouth grew dry as he chanted the mantra just below his breath, hypnotically: "You're dead, Maddy.")

But the swings still swung and Maddy still grasped the chains, as annoyingly *there* as ever.

Then Robbie heard his whispers, heard his words and stopped. Guilt swept down slow and heavy from his forehead to his chest, pushing his eyes closed as it went. What was he doing? Maddy was annoying, but she didn't deserve what Jimmy got. Nobody deserved what Jimmy got.

And it didn't work, anyway. Robbie clenched his fists and pounded the dirt beside him. It didn't work! Maybe he was crazy. Maybe he needed more practice. Or maybe the hole just wouldn't show up with so many witnesses. With Jimmy it had waited until Robbie was the only watcher. It *had* waited, hadn't it? How could it have *known?*

He was relieved that it did know, somehow. He never should have dared it to take Maddy. The guilt spread through his chest and encased his heart like a thick sleeve of oil. Something Mrs. Fricks had said in Sunday school came back, in pieces. Some proverb about fools venting anger. He didn't want to be a fool, and he nearly had been just now.

He would need to be more careful, that's all. Keep himself in check.

As long as he did that, what could happen?

ARGON

Gossip is a lovely poison much like alcohol: enjoyable in small doses but ever so sinister when taking you under its spell. It inhibits and inhabits the lady and man alike, twisting gentle slander into violent and sometimes everlasting scars. It is idle talk, ruthless rumour, the all-inclusive folly of the world, and takes from all it touches a sliver of the bleeding soul.

And its beginnings often are murky because it starts as innocent conversation.

The conversation begins on this night with an exchange between husband and wife, as it has a billion times before. Kevin and Susanna in bed, she with a book, he with a deep understanding that what he was about to tell her would kill any chance of bedroom fun. Walt was her father, after all, and even if he was right about Robbie Larsen (though the times Kevin had truly agreed with his father-in-law were few, indeed, and this wasn't one of them), Kevin knew that the mere mention of family in bed was enough to maim the most carefully crafted mood. Even though Susanna usually sided with him in Walt-Kevin disagreements, the weight of the conflicts inflicted emotional pressure sores that rarely faded by morning.

But if Walt talked to her tomorrow—talked to her *first*—that seed might set her mind in Walt's direction. Perhaps not, but for Kevin, looking for an edge over Walt's ramrod ways had grown into a habit.

He bit the bullet and rolled toward Sue, and told her of Walt and Robbie's confrontation, Thomas's intervention, and his own nagging disgust that he hadn't shoved Walt's theory from his mind. Robbie couldn't *possibly* have had anything to do with Jimmy's disappearance . . .

Susanna fell asleep that night with Robbie's bloody hands glowing in her mind.

∞ ∞ ∞

Wilfred Wight didn't like Blackwell much, but he did know one thing: the man was as sharp as he was gruff. He'd been bang on many times before about things people and political, and when Walt Blackwell set his mind on something, it was usually headed for the finish line (and rumour had it he was finally thinking of running for the mayor's chair). He wasn't foolproof, but Blackwell was usually a pretty good gauge for what the people thought—or would think, once they heard him talking. This was a regular source of consternation for Wight as mayor, but he'd grown slowly accustomed to holding his nose and using Blackwell as a political weather vane.

The most frustrating part of all, of course, was that Blackwell would get the credit even if Wight ended up doing the legwork once the people decided they wanted Walt's idea. If history held true, it wouldn't be long before Blackwell spread his theory and got people asking Wight to look into *this* one. This time, though, if Wight played it right, he could launch a preemptive strike and take the rightful credit for the legwork to follow.

Blackwell presumed the Richmond boy's disappearance was "no accident". So what was behind it, then? Or rather, who? Sure, some of his fellow citizens rubbed him the wrong way, but there wasn't a man or woman he knew in Argon capable of taking a child . . . no one he knew well, but that was Walt's point, he supposed.

Wight rummaged through the kitchen drawer where Elsie kept the notepads and pulled out a junior-sized with three cats on the cover. He smiled. Cute. He'd sit a bit, jot down some of the town's newest names (maybe run them past Elsie), and set things straight before

Blackwell took his lunch again.

The missile had left its launch pad.

What Wight forgot was that Elsie (young though she was in a way that only forty-five years of marriage can see) was in with all the oldest lips in town. Generous lips that would share what they learned before the sound had settled in their deafening ears. It wasn't their fault, he'd think if he mulled it over awhile. Agnes was a sweetie and couldn't help being sociable. Bernice bought friends and talk was currency. And Georgina . . . well, for all the words Georgina knew, she never had learned *confidential*.

Wight may as well have handed them his thoughts and a bullhorn.

∞ ∞ ∞

Susanna hadn't *meant* to tell.

She woke Thursday with the vague uneasiness that follows a forgotten nightmare, but lost it in her morning routine before the five-forty key at the Country Rose. Breakfast at six on weekdays (five-fifty-five for Silas and Wesley Hoffman most mornings, the quiet bachelors from up River Road who had already tended the cows and probably fixed a fence or two).

Not long after she set plates in front of the Hoffman boys, the breakfast rush turned furious. Busy days weren't uncommon, but even claimed tables usually had an empty seat or two. Not today. A lot of folks seemed to guess the province's search team would choose the Rose for a quick bite before resuming their duties, and the group of twelve proved them right at ten past six. The din dropped to a buzz as they claimed the last three tables of four—loud enough to skirt suspicion of eavesdropping but quiet enough to overhear if one of the search crew said something important.

Sue called Veronica after ten minutes of wishing Kevin was there to help and a growing realization that she wasn't keeping up. She felt guilty calling for help in the middle of her sister-in-law's grief, but maybe it wasn't all bad. Maybe a change of pace would get Ronnie's mind off the search awhile.

It wouldn't, though, and Sue knew it. No mother could get her mind off a missing child any more than she could tear out her heart and toss it away. Life was different, and no amount of distraction would change that. Bless Ronnie's heart for saying yes, but Sue realized while almost burning Cliff Pembrooke's slab of ham that the last thing Ronnie needed was to walk through a room full of people searching for her child. Sue called back and told her to use the rear door.

Even with Ronnie standing silent over the stoves, the rush challenged Sue's "ten minutes to the table" personal motto. Once the search crew arrived, she bumped their orders to the front of the list. They had the most important work to get to of anyone there, and it was the most practical way she could think up to help Ronnie right now.

Nobody complained. Maybe they were just too interested in gleaning new info from the search crew without the risk of killing the atmosphere by asking, but in a brief and overwhelming moment of emotion after returning through the swinging kitchen door to near privacy, Sue loved them for their patience.

By seven-thirty, the mountain of orders had dwindled to a prairie flat line: mostly level, with an occasional rut or speed bump. If the search and rescue team had given up any critical information before leaving their generous tip, Sue hadn't heard, which troubled her. She liked to hear what her diners were saying as much to clear up any later misinformation as to settle her own curiosity; she'd lived in Argon all her life and knew what a small town could do with a single misrepresented idea.

So it was merely accidental that she described what she heard from Kevin about Jimmy's friend, Robbie. Well, what she heard from Kevin was more about her father than Robbie, but it didn't come out that way as she spoke with Ronnie in the small kitchen as the smell of bacon grease soaked in their hair. Or perhaps Ronnie just didn't seem to hear it that way. Yes, that was probably it.

Guilt nagged Sue like a crumb of 12-grain lodged between molars as she finished her story. She had to finish it, even though she could see in Ronnie's eyes that telling hadn't been a good idea to start with. But she wasn't telling just *anybody*. Ronnie was Kevin's sister and he probably would have told her soon, anyway—and as Jimmy's mother, Ronnie deserved to know.

Susanna tried to believe that, but couldn't ignore the dreadful sense settling on her that as Jimmy's mother, Ronnie was probably the last person she should have told.

∞ ∞ ∞

"Oh, I feel so bad for them. He's been gone for two days now. I'm really starting to worry for Veronica!"

"Isn't it terrible? I can't *imagine* how terrible she must feel."

"Things happen. Kids get too close to the water and—whoop—off they go."

"Where were his parents? Tsk. Someone should have been watching."

"Isn't it terrible? I can't *imagine* how terrible she must feel!"

"Have you talked to her?"

"Well . . . no."

"Search and Rescue haven't found anything yet. They've checked the whole town!"

"If he was just lost, I think they would have found him already."

"You think he *wanted* to leave? Like maybe Terry and Ronnie were beating him?"

"My boy did *not* run away! Someone took him."

"Ja hear what Walt thinks? Was gettin' th' oil checked an' he said nob'dy's come roun' here for mont's."

"Months, I know. That's what I heard. It *has* to be someone from town!"

"The Larsens? Yes, I met them at church. Why?"

"He's not from here, you know. They left the States to get away. When people change countries, it's to escape something. Or if it's for better opportunities, why wouldn't they move to the city?"

"My uncle's brother's sister-in-law is a border guard, did you know that? Not at this crossing, but in Windygates. She says they entered the country through Windygates. That's more than an hour away, but a lot quieter. Now why would they avoid the crossing that's right next to where they're moving?"

"Does anyone know what he does for a living? What the hell kinda whack job works on the In'ernet?"

"She told me herself this summer, while I did her hair: they haven't settled anywhere in *years*. But she didn't say why . . ."

"No, nothing like this ever happened before. Not until *they* arrived."

"As a professional, I'm just saying. Her hair . . . could use some work."

FIVE

Whispers grow loud quickly in small spaces, where the echo of rumours is measured in hours, not days.

Thomas had seen his name written in accusatory eyes since Thursday as he assisted three separate search parties in and out of Argon, and he was beginning to feel that the search was becoming as important for his family's well-being as for Jimmy's. But in the two days since Search and Rescue took over Argon Fire Hall, not a single shred of Jimmy's whereabouts had been found.

Friday afternoon was cool as Thomas walked his course in the human dragnet stretching across the Plummer field east of town, but he recognized the slow burn building in his head as he considered the growing suspicion directed his way. He shook his head to clear the sensation and drew a long breath. Anger was the last thing he needed to embrace right now. He disliked the sudden negative attention but he understood it well: people were scared and had a right to be, and new families were low-hanging fruit that fearful people liked to pluck.

That, and Blackwell. Thomas would bet the land he was walking that Blackwell was lead plucker. Thomas shook off the tiny tingling in his forehead again, the one that always preceded the burn; he couldn't let his anger take over right now. Not now, not ever. He'd kept it at bay for so long and transformed his entire approach to people—to life—to make sure his emotions wouldn't control him again. He'd learned far too young how lashing out in anger or fear or uncertainty could hurt those around him. His response mattered, and he had sworn to craft careful responses to even the most infuriating situations. And he had succeeded, counting each day of thousands since the last time his anger broke free.

Thomas dug his hand into his jeans pocket and retrieved the 1804 half dollar tucked inside. The half had helped. He'd gazed often into Lady Liberty's eye in times of weakness to recall a momentary strength: *An angry man is half a man,* his mother had told him the day she gave him the coin. *Just like this. Looks beautiful, but it'll never be a dollar.*

He slid the coin back into his pocket and stepped over a pile of trampled spring wheat discarded during harvest. Twenty feet over, Mellie formed the next link in the human chain sweeping the field for any sign of missing Jimmy Richmond. Thomas sighed. He knew the burden she felt over Jimmy being gone and her own kids still carrying on . . . the guilt of walking them to school and not seeing Ronnie walking her boy. But carrying on was necessary. The children of Argon needed routine to assure them that the lies their parents told were true:

We'll find Jimmy soon.
Everything will be okay.

All kids need lies from their parents sometimes—the kind God might overlook because He knows everyone just needs a little protection sometimes. Robbie and Bec needed that now, too. Thomas knew it and he knew Mellie knew it, but that didn't ease the devastation of the truth they hid: that carrying on was lunacy.

He wouldn't infect the search effort with that idea. Three days in, the collective confidence of the searchers was an eggshell—still intact, still guarding the hope tucked inside, but sensitive to the slightest pressure. Once the first voice struck its blow of hopelessness, the entire facade would crumble.

He and Mellie would continue searching. They would have anyway, to show their new neighbours that they were here for the long haul, that they cared. But with whispers pointing in their direction, they couldn't dare stop now. They couldn't add any fuel to the fire Thomas sensed beneath the surface of their neighbours' strained stares.

He looked to his right again at Mellie and smiled slightly. She would speak her mind to him tonight, but out here she would keep walking, keep searching; keep *helping,* as though she believed. And he knew she wasn't doing it for the people around them as much as she was doing it for him.

∞ ∞ ∞

Mellie checked the hand-carved clock on the kitchen wall and sighed. She had known this morning that the day would run late due to searching, so had allowed Bec to go to Maddy's house after school. Maddy's house was just off the school grounds—across the street and across the school field from their own home—and Maddy's mother's kitchen window overlooked the field enough to assure Mellie that the kids would be fine.

But Bec was supposed to have come home by five, and the long hand on the province-shaped clock was starting to flatten due east. Mellie hadn't liked the play date idea with all that had happened this week, but that was more from the busyness and tension than a fear of what might happen. Her instinct told her that Jimmy's disappearance was no kidnapping. Sometimes kids wandered and got snatched by the world around them—by rivers or caverns . . . or things unknown.

The unknown she had lived with and learned to accept (for herself). Accepting it for her daughter was a much more difficult matter, though she agreed with Thomas (but still hated when he reminded her) that they couldn't just keep their kids trapped inside. The more Bec faced life directly, the sooner she would learn to deal. Survival was *all about* learning to live with what life gave you, despite the distress that could follow.

And follow it had.

Mellie stirred the sauce in the Crock-Pot and coated the chicken with another layer of honey barbecue glaze. With each move from city to town, she felt more and more like that chicken breast swimming. Swimming *at first,* then struggling against the thickening force of despair until it congealed around her, suffocating her in an inescapable situation.

She liked the idea of the tiny town set in the sprawling country, but the truth of it wasn't practical. Some people were friendlier than in past stops but others were nosier. People ignore newcomers in cities (she had learned), notice them in middling towns, and downright inspect them in burgs like Argon. The default mistrust in people's eyes seemed to grow stronger as the populations dwindled. Maybe the mistrust was equal everywhere, but it *felt different* here—especially this week. That was another reason why she'd approved the play date: she was afraid Bec wouldn't get many more, the way people were talking lately.

She worried most for Bec. Robbie would be okay, but Bec was

different. She'd been born with a streak of her father in her—the dangerous streak he'd pushed down for so many years. Mellie knew how strong Thomas had had to be to keep it in check—how could they expect Bec to navigate her emotions when they uprooted her so frequently? She was so young to be given such responsibility, and with such an unstable foundation.

Mellie brushed her hand against the inside of the Crock-Pot and howled from the searing heat. She slammed the wooden spoon on the counter and regretted it instantly as the spoon sprayed a brown arc of honey barbecue against her like a skunk warding off an attacker. She howled again, not from pain but frustration, and clamped her mouth shut before her thoughts could tumble out. Robbie was in the next room, after all.

"You okay, Mom?"

She allowed herself a half-smile despite her frustration. Even when immersed in his video games, he still cared. That was the other streak she saw in Thomas, the one she hadn't been able to resist all those years ago. "I'll be all right. Thanks, honey." Then, as she wet a cloth to rescue her top, "Robbie, supper will be ready soon. Can you please get your sister and bring her home?"

He growled a little. "Can't you just phone Maddy's house?"

She stopped dabbing at her shirt and peered through the kitchen doorway with stern eyes. "Tone, Robbie. And they'll probably be out in the field or at the playground."

"What!" He was out the front door the next moment, jumping on his bike and pedalling with a fury that only the young or frightened can maintain. Strewn in his wake, a jumble of games and controllers on the floor next to the perfectly useful, but empty, organizer basket.

Mellie sighed again and resumed dabbing.

∞ ∞ ∞

Robbie couldn't feel his legs but could gauge how hard they were pumping by the force of wind through his hair. Another time, this could have been one of those classic summer moments: biking so fast as though he were flying; sharp blast of air on his face, cold tears forming in the corners of his eyes; going full tilt until his lungs nearly burst from exertion.

But for the fear of what lay ahead.

He flew across the street without checking for traffic, ignoring all thought of cars or kids or creatures straggling. One image alone flashed in his mind—the thing that had swallowed Jimmy—and as he pedalled he tried to will the thing away from his sister. His baby sister, who didn't suspect a thing.

The playground was close—down a short dirt path between the two-storey homes across from Robbie's house. A large grass field, where kids played everything from pick-up soccer to semi-organized baseball, stretched from the fence at the end of the path to the north edge of the school building. The playground sprawled across its sand patch forty feet from the school's east doors.

Most of the playground was new, thanks to provincial supplements that brought the old development a few decades closer to code. Three styles of monkey bars surrounded the structure, close enough together that the big kids could avoid the ground indefinitely. A climbing wall with choice of rope or rubber rocks towered over children of all ages. The old metal slide had been replaced by two plastic ones at opposite corners of the sand: softer, safer, less likely to draw blood (when they weren't busy consuming children).

When he arrived at the playground, Robbie spotted his sister's bike immediately: black frame, pink striping, silver tassels on the handlebars. Just like Bec—mostly tomboy with a bit of dolls and tea parties mixed in.

Robbie threw his own bike aside carelessly and shouted her name, trying to keep his voice calm against the rising wind. An errant tune whistled through the trees and something creaked nearby: the ancient merry-go-round, throwback to an era when injury lawyers were sparse and common sense was plentiful.

He thought again of Jimmy and his throat went dry.

His next shout came out a squeak and he cleared his throat before calling again, to no response. No one was playing on the field. The swings were empty. The playground was silent.

Bec was gone.

His sister's bike—and now he could see Maddy's through the fire pole drop on the other side of the structure—was the only sign that anyone had been here. How much had he missed her by? An hour? A minute?

Robbie's stomach turned as he wondered what to tell his parents. His eyes dampened and he called out again with a hoarse scream.

Then he heard giggling and his fear turned to fury in an instant. Maddy's head poked around the back edge of the large slide's covered entrance, followed by Bec's head, then Roseli's. Robbie shouted his sister's name again, this time with venom.

"That's not funny, you runt!" He ran toward the slide and she retreated behind the bright plastic wall. "You're late for supper. Come on."

No response.

"Fine. I'm going back. Mom's going to be mad."

Her toes poked out from the covered top, pointing down the slide, just like Jimmy's before he slid away. The other girls were holed up in the entry tunnel with no line of sight to the bottom of the slide.

There were no witnesses. *It was going to happen again.*

"Wait!"

Bec giggled again and launched herself forward, arms stretched to the sky.

"No!" Robbie sprinted full bore and leaped onto the hard plastic runway at the bottom of the slide. He tried to scoop Bec up as she slid into him, but her momentum knocked him backward. They tangled into a heap in the sand, with Robbie landing hard on top of his sister. Bec flailed at him and yelled until he rolled off. He looked around for any sign of what had taken Jimmy, but saw only Roseli and Maddy approaching.

"Are you okay?" Roseli asked.

Bec stood and wiped sand from her hair. "Yeah." She glared at her brother. "You're so mean!" She said goodbye to her friends and retrieved her bike. "Wait till I tell Mom!"

She shot off for home and her friends followed. Maddy stared back at Robbie, mirroring Bec's disgust.

Robbie watched the girls pedal away and inhaled sharply. He hadn't meant to scare his sister, but she wouldn't believe that. Would his parents?

His hands shook as he lifted his bike from the ground. A tear trickled along the edge of his nose. He would have to tell them what he had seen. This was his home now, these were his friends. The slide had taken Jimmy without warning. What if it wasn't finished?

The adults would know what to do. In any case, he needed a clear conscience if it happened again.

There was no way through this but to tell.

∞ ∞ ∞

"And then he *attacked* her!" Maddy could hardly contain her glee. She was an only child and resented her parents for not having produced a sibling to torment. Long ago she had decided that those of her friends would suffice.

Maddy's mother raised an eyebrow. "Aren't you glad you don't have a brother, dear?"

"And Bec didn't even *do* anything! We were just playing. She went down the slide and he went crazy!"

Maddy's father hated the tattling, but resisted the urge to tell her to shut up. He was a good dad, or tried to be. "Finish your supper, Maddy."

"Jumped on her and wouldn't let her go. When he finally did, he chased her all the way home."

"Oh, my!"

"Finish your supper."

"I can't believe he would *do* that!"

"Finish. Your. Supper."

Maddy's mother scooped up the last of her meal and stood, still chewing. "You wash the dishes, Jonathan. I have some phone calls to make."

SIX

"You know what I think?" Mellie said as she slung another rake load of leaves into the orange lawn bag. "I think this place is going to kill me."

Thomas emitted a sharp laugh. "That's not what you said when you first saw it."

Mellie's eyes swept across the massive yard, from the oaks lining the west border and south along Park Street to the long, dirt driveway unfurling from the narrow break in the trees two hundred feet toward their new home. The large house was a neighbourhood oddity, the sole building still standing since the Great War. It stood at the back of a large lot in the elbow of the curved street, its stubborn weather-beaten stones defying the call of a new century.

"If I'd given this more thought, I probably would have realized that a big yard means big work. At least in the city we could have hired someone."

"That's why we have kids." Thomas grinned, sending sparks like blue diamonds through his eyes.

"Yeah, and one's still dawdling her way home to avoid the tough stuff. I doubt they'll be the difference makers you think they'll be."

He stopped raking and freed a leaf from her blonde locks. "I distinctly remember someone mentioning the phrase 'dream home' when we looked at it. That was you, wasn't it?"

"Reality's never the same. I always forget that in the moment." She flashed a playful smile. "I don't even want to think about tackling that cellar!"

He grunted in agreement. "It'll be fine, hon. We don't have to finish it all today."

He was right, of course, but right then, Mellie didn't care if they even finished the front lawn. They were together, and they were *alone*. After four days of little rest, the searchers had all agreed that they needed to recharge in shifts, and give more time to themselves and their families than they had for the better part of the week. They would rejoin the search later that day, but for now . . . no neighbours and not even their own kids in sight, what with Bec still at Grinbergs and Robbie working the back yard. If they could enjoy more moments like these, well . . . maybe this place could work.

"We won't finish at all at the rate you're going, mister." Mellie scooped up another batch of burgundy and apple-yellow leaves, leaned close, and whispered teasingly in Thomas's ear. "Open up that bag."

∞ ∞ ∞

Robbie slammed his rake down in the pile of back yard leaves he'd spent the last ten minutes gathering. Bec should have been home a half hour ago. She *knew* they had yard chores this morning.

She wouldn't be much help at six years old, of course, but the principle bothered him. The little runt always pushed, and usually got away with it. And now while he cleaned the back yard on his own, she was out with her friends.

He reached down and fumbled for the rake pole under the leaves while trying to calm himself. He was just tired. He had fought sleep the night before as he thought of how to tell his parents what he knew about Jimmy's disappearance. No matter how many conversations he played out, he couldn't convince himself that any made sense. How would he convince *them*?

He hissed a hard breath through pursed lips, then dragged the rake toward his feet and shook the clinging leaves into the growing pile. He'd always thought of raking as one of the worst side effects of the Fall. The Eden he'd seen in Sunday school picture books (regardless of where his family moved) was always flush with varied shades of green, not autumn colours, and while the reds and oranges and yellows made for the most beautiful season each year, he thought there must be a reason you never saw autumn in the picture books. Had leaves died in Eden?

Work was a curse borne of the Fall—well, he would swear up and down that this was the case, even though his mom said it wasn't work so much as *what happened to work* that was the curse. Made it dull, repetitive. Unnecessary. Nothing worse than dull, repetitive, *unnecessary* work. Like raking.

Even though the turn of the leaves wowed him each year and the float of the first to the ground gave him hope that change didn't have to mean an end to beauty, there was something symbolic about dragging the stiffening, crisp corpses toward himself; standing in the center of the dead, drawing them to himself to purge them from his life for another year (when everyone knew that leaving them to rot was probably better for the yard). Couldn't they just mulch them all and be done with it? Ashes to dust and all that. Wasn't *that* in the Bible, or was it just a cliché movie line? He'd have to ask Mrs. Fricks about that, too.

He drew another clump of leaves inward and looked up when a flick of movement caught his eye. Out beyond the yard, up along the decades-old dike that separated the homes on Park Street from the winding Red River, Bec and Roseli were running. He scrunched his face in disgust. There she was! He shouted Bec's name but neither girl turned. His disgusted scrunch deepened to a scowl. He threw the rake down into the leaf pile again and sprinted toward the edge of the yard past the near-empty vegetable garden, then megaphoned his hands around his mouth to howl his sister's name.

Again, she ignored him. In one regrettable millisecond, he wished the slide had taken Bec instead of Jimmy on Tuesday. He pushed the thought away instantly, then ignored his shame long enough to entertain the fantasy. *Not Bec, but maybe Roseli at least. If Bec didn't have her stupid friend to play with, she'd be* here *right now.*

He watched Bec and Roseli as they raced atop the dike, and overlaid the ghostly image of Tuesday's memory like a video editor mixing footage. There was Jimmy, bounding across the swinging bridge again

and Roseli running, thirty feet ahead of Bec, easy

Jimmy ducking into the launch pad

Roseli shifting course, turning toward the far side of the dike

Jimmy sliding with that darned goofy smile

Roseli dipping below the crest line

(poof)

gone.

Bec shouted at Roseli in a tone that was anything but playful. That's when Robbie noticed that she wasn't just skipping along like her usual carefree self. Even from his back yard, Robbie saw the etch of intensity—and anger—on her face and he realized suddenly that she wasn't just running with her friend along the dike. She was running *after* her.

He yelled Bec's name over and over, his voice growing more urgent and frustrated each time, but the words seemed to die in the dainty breeze. When he grew tired of shouting, he scoffed and waved her off with both hands. *Let them fight.* Maybe it would end their play date sooner than she'd planned. That would teach her to disobey Mom—and leave all the yard work for *him*.

∞ ∞ ∞

"He is *not!*" Bec shouted as Roseli burst through the chain link gate and ran to the base of the dike behind the Grinberg home. "Take that back!" Bec ran to the gate and pushed hard before it could swing all the way back to its latch. The gate bounced off her small hand and the opening widened enough for her to slip through. "He is *not* a meanie!"

The girls had been playing in the small back yard fort Trent had constructed over the summer using the remains of a picnic table and the sides of cardboard appliance boxes he had gathered from neighbours. The craftsmanship was of pre-teen quality, but sturdy enough for the safety stamp of approval from his dad ("as long as you're not playing out there in a windstorm," he'd said).

Bec and Roseli were playing Town with their dolls and some of Trent's old cars and action figures they had found stored in the basement. They had developed quite the booming township, complete with the hockey rink on Main and Morris and Georgie's Chinese restaurant on Taylor with the three-room hotel on the second level. (It was missing the low-lit backroom bar some locals used when they weren't crossing the border for a cheap restock at Happy Harry's, but the girls lived in blissful ignorance of what the posters touting Miss Kitty's next appearance really meant. The sign in the restaurant's shared lobby said NO ONE OVER 18 ADMITTED, and that was all they had to know about *that*.)

Trouble was, Roseli overdid the realism just a tad, and after Bec drove the Larsen's Hot Wheels '64 Vette through the pumps at Walt's Wrench & Gas, Walt himself (back when he was really the black-hooded Snake Eyes of G.I. Joe fame) whispered something not meant to be retold.

Something about the Larsens.

Bec chased Roseli up the south side of the dike, reached the top and was sprinting forward when she realized she still clutched a Cabbage Patch doll (one of Susanna Grinberg's old favourites) in her hands. Up until Snake Eyes's slip of the tongue at the gas pump, the Patch had been an effective stand-in for Bec's mom, who (naturally) took great offence to the silent ninja's statement.

Bec tossed the doll aside—partly because she wanted more speed and partly because it belonged to that dirty double-crosser Roseli— and charged down the dirt path atop the dike. There were two worn strips (tire tracks, really, from years of use by Argon's maintenance truck) that summer's imagination often transformed into a race track. Many days, brightly coloured blurs would cycle along the dirt paths in search of glory, after which the noisy winners and losers alike would head to the public swimming pool for a dip or the canteen for ice cream.

Bec ran hard, watching the gap close between herself and Roseli but wishing anyway that she had her bike to catch up faster. And wishing she hadn't thrown away the Mellie Patch Kid, because now what would she do when she caught Roseli? She wasn't going to *hit* her, was she? She had only wanted to stand up for her family name, maybe scare Roseli a little before making up and going back for more Town. Tossing the doll in Roseli's direction would have sent the perfect message without going too far.

Now, all Bec had were her hands. The same small hands currently balled into tight fists and tick-tocking back and forth like the metronome at Mrs. Granpierre's piano lessons. Bec loved that metronome tucked in its wooden pyramid. It settled her like nothing else in her six years had, save for the sound of her mother's soothing voice. And while her burst of anger had propelled her from her sitting position in the Grinberg back yard into a *moderato* starting pace, she had *allegretto'd* quickly and skipped *allegro* and *vivace* altogether to reach her current *presto* pace in record time.

Roseli shifted from the left tire track after stumbling on a rut on the roadway, and skipped over the right dirt strip to the grassy shoulder. But she wasn't stopping there. No, she was tracking down the slope toward the riverside forest that clustered all along the Red.

Bec yelled at her friend to stop. Why was she going there? There was nothing safe on that side of the dike. Bec's parents had cautioned her several times over the summer never to visit the Other Side. Not without them, anyway. There were too many dangers lurking—snakes, raccoons, foxes, the thick of the forest, the pull of the Red. But today she would have to try, and her parents would understand. She had to protect the family name, and now protect Roseli herself (who was laughing a little now, as though she hadn't heard how dangerous the Other Side could be). Bec could still yell at her, scare her a little, then bring her back up to safety and head back for tea in Town.

Bec heard a shout that sounded like her brother's as she started down the dike toward the riverside forest. Instinct turned her head and she looked over her shoulder, though she had scaled too far down to see anything on the other side. The Safe Side.

The sky darkened abruptly as the taller trees blotted out the sun, and Bec turned back in a jolt of panic to face the forest again. She became aware suddenly of razor thin blades of grass slapping at her ankles, and the air gushing in from the field around her like saltwater waves heavy in her nostrils. Panic set in, and her feet stopped as though glued to the ground, or perhaps her laces had wound around her shoes and burrowed into the dirt. She *couldn't* go any farther. Why did Roseli have to run down this side where she was not allowed?

Robbie shouted again from the other side, fainter now, but Bec tensed at the sound of his voice. Had he seen her cross the boundary their parents had set? What if he told them?

Her parents! Mom had told her to be back for chores and Bec had forgotten while playing Town with Roseli. Which explained Robbie's tone. And if Robbie was angry, then of course he'd tell their parents. Bec's breathing shortened and her throat constricted.

Birds fluttered up (strangely silent) from the trees at the base of the dike, as though responding to a hunter's shot. Then she realized the birds, flapping their way to the nearest clouds for cover, were all that moved. Roseli wasn't running anymore. Bec couldn't see her anywhere.

Roseli was gone.

∞ ∞ ∞

Roseli slapped the first birch of the forest as if it were a friend high-fiving. She laughed as she sprang into the thicket and left the grass slope behind. Bec wouldn't find her in here; not while she was so angry, anyway. So angry over something so silly. What did it matter if her grandpa had said mean things about Bec's dad? That was adult stuff, and a waste of time. They had more important things to take care of, like Town.

While running along the dike, Roseli could feel Bec getting closer. (When Bec's family moved in, it had only taken until the second week for the girls to figure out that Bec was faster. Not the fastest of their friends, but faster than Roseli for sure.) Bec's steady footsteps slapped off-beat echoes behind her, but it was Bec's sharp voice that scared her more. She didn't think Bec would hurt her, but the shorter the gap between them became, the more Roseli worried about what Bec *would* do when she caught up. Roseli realized she'd never seen Bec get angry (upset at dumb big brother stuff didn't count) and she began to wonder whether Bec angry might be better off avoided.

So she ran down the far side of the dike. She knew her friend wasn't allowed on the Other Side, as Bec called it, because she'd played with Bec much of the summer and knew the Larsen's rules inside out. Many were the same as her own house rules, but she thought that one was a little weird. It wasn't like the river came up near the dike; there was a small forest and a clay riverbank between the dike and the river's edge. The Larsens hadn't grown up with a river behind them, though, so Roseli figured water just scared them. She knew if you played safe (and didn't always tell your parents where you'd been), there was nothing to be worried about. At least, that is, until flooding season.

She knew Bec wouldn't follow her to the forest, but she hadn't looked back to see whether Bec was still following her until she reached the first tree. When she turned, she saw Bec standing a few steps down the dike, looking over her shoulder like a squirrel checking for spies as it hid its last nut. Scared of the river, just like her parents.

Pine needles scraped the top of Roseli's head as she ducked under a snapped and dangling branch. She could wait out Bec's anger for a few minutes, then head back to the tiny pumps at G.I. Walt's Wrench & Gas to clean up.

Then the ground opened up under her without warning.

∞ ∞ ∞

Bec stared down to the forest edge, watching the grass rise slowly in the little spots where Roseli's rubber boots had tramped through. Could she have made it to the forest so quickly? It was at least twenty, thirty . . . okay, she didn't know how far (Mrs. Beauchamp's kindergarten class still worked with carrots for units of length, and Bec only knew that her arm was two shorts or one long, counting the greens), but it was *so* far from where she stood. The thought of walking down all that way made her shiver.

Bec's soles popped free of the ground and she set a foot forward. She was wearing runners, not rubbers, and had already gotten them mucky, which would *not* impress her mom. But she couldn't stop now. She'd all but forgotten about protecting the family name—she needed to find Roseli.

Bec set another foot forward and her stomach turned at the thought of what might lie waiting behind the trees. A wolf? A bear? Perhaps a python up in the branches . . . or whatever had scared away the birds.

Then Robbie shouted again and a flare exploded somewhere in her head in a burst of anger toward him for knowing she was breaking the rules, and toward Roseli for dragging her here to the scary side— the rule-breaking side. The flare blasted out from behind her eyes like fireworks in July, and she winced as the day brightened from its canvas of blue, green, and brown into a sheet of perfect white. The sky, the grass, the trees all vanished from her sight, leaving only brilliant specks of firework orange dripping down the white sheet like liquid fire on paper.

Bec's eyes rolled up as though tugged by string, like the marionettes at the summer festival her family had attended in Franklin Falls. Her thoughts of Roseli vanished like the day had as her eyes rolled back further in her head. She couldn't feel the grass anymore or the wind pressing her nose and throat, just heard echoes of Robbie's call and knew she had to get back to the top of the dike. The Other Side was angry.

She stumbled up—she thought she felt *up*—then the white sheet went black and she saw only the orange drops burning, leading her on like fireflies in the middle of the darkest day. The orange specks flitted in her vision and shrank as she ran (was she still running now, or floating?), dissipating into the darkness and shrieking at her with the overlapping voices of Robbie and Roseli. Then the last of the fireflies blinked out, and she fell forward into the darkness as the marionette strings tugged her eyes the rest of the short distance into the back of her head.

∞ ∞ ∞

Roseli clung to the trunk of a birch, squealing and crying Bec's name—Bec had been right behind her during the chase, and had even started down the dike after her. Where had she gone?

Roseli craned her neck to look over her shoulder and down to her feet, which were submerged in the ground, or rather in a sort of liquid hole that had opened up in the ground. The hole was dark as shadow, like a pool of painted death that spread unopposed. She squealed louder as the hole swelled past her ankles (one bare, the other still booted) and up to her shins, stretching wider with every skip of her heart. She had slid from her horizontal position on the forest earth, now dangling and lacing her fingertips around back of the tree trunk as the ground disappeared slowly beneath her. The hole crawled past her stomach, her chest, and finally (her squeals at their highest pitch now, though muffled by the papery bark against her cheek), her head.

She hung from the trunk, dangling into the dark, featureless pit. There were no dirt walls to brace her, nothing to kick against or on which to get a foothold. All she could do was hold on to the base of the birch and keep screaming. Any moment now, Bec would appear at the edge of this nightmare with her dad—she was taking so long because she went to get her dad! Of this Roseli was becoming quite certain—and they would wake her up and pull her to safety.

But no one came, and the hole kept growing. The darkness ate away at the ground beneath Roseli, flowing under her birch now and wiping away the forest floor like a felt eraser on whiteboard ink. The tree shifted as the abyss opened around her, then groaned as the expanse opened its jaw wider—just a little wider to force the tree to shudder and bow like helianthus to the sun. The birch didn't crack, but she heard a popping sound like the time Trent's shoulder came out of its socket when he fell from the old tree house the previous summer (the tree house their father dismantled the very next weekend at their mother's firm request). The birch tore free of its roots as though they were cobwebs, sending the snake-like tendrils pinging back into the soil.

Roseli screamed again as the tree's middle slammed the edge of the hole, jarring her loose and leaving her scrambling to lock her fingers around the trunk as the birch slid down into the hole, *under the ground,* surrounding her with the darkness of a galaxy without stars.

Then she was falling like Trent the year before . . . she looked up and watched the world fade away through the hole (that now appeared to be closing). Blackness surrounded her, broken only by the dimming white of her birch and a shrinking dot of blue sky hardly visible through the tops of the remaining trees. She opened her mouth to scream once more but the darkness swallowed the sound before it could begin.

Then the emptiness took her, blotting out the blue dot as the hole melted into itself. Roseli fell, terrified and silent, gripping the birch like a life preserver in an ocean of darkness.

SEVEN

The first thing Kevin Grinberg did when he discovered his daughter was missing was call the RCMP.

Wade Slater (Wes's barely teen boy with a hook nose and an attitude) had sneaked his dad's quad out to the dike while Wes helped a search team along the riverside brush north of Highway 200. Wade found Bec Larsen lying atop the dike near the treatment plant just off the river and a skipped stone away from Main and Morris, and brought the groggy girl home with a careful ride back through town to Park Street. Bec seemed fine but short on details—Roseli was nowhere to be seen and Bec had only a vague sense of an argument they'd had. She couldn't even remember where the girls had been playing.

After an unsuccessful search of the dike and school grounds, Kevin asked Sergeant Gilford to post constables at Argon's primary choke points while he rallied a search crew. Roseli hadn't been missing for long and other teams were already sweeping the golf course and nearby fields outside town limits for days-old signs of Jimmy Richmond. The local detachment wasn't large enough to cordon off the whole town, but they could monitor the exit routes for a kidnapper. Yes, a *kidnapper,* he told Gilford. Screw Wight and his fear of scaring parents, it was time to be realistic.

(In private conversation, at least, and only to light a fire under Gilford. Kevin had to admit the kidnapper theme was still a terrible idea to let loose in public.)

He stood atop Argon's west dike in the place where Wade Slater found Bec, staring down grim-faced at the bank of the river. To his left, the old black rail bridge stretched across the Red, its large concrete piles a favourite meeting place for teen daredevils who would climb down through the tracks to hide in the pile housing above the rushing river. A perfect place for experimentation, as long as no one got so high that they couldn't find their way out.

Three dozen men and women gathered around Kevin after responding to his urgent call, an agglomeration buzzing with questions and theories of what had happened. Blackwell had just suggested searching homes when Kevin quieted the group. "She's lost, not kidnapped."

Blackwell raised one eyebrow. "You sound fairly certain of that."

Kevin was far from certain, but he had the people's ear and didn't want to be reckless. "Look, nobody new has come through here in months. You know as well as I do that the gossip line's been dry on that account." His voice took on an edge. "They haven't stopped whispering about Angad and Tom's families yet because they haven't had anyone else new to talk about."

Someone snorted. Thomas, in the thick of the crowd, failed at suppressing a smile.

Kevin continued. "I can't imagine a kidnapper feeling safe enough to stick around this long after—" his voice trailed off as he noticed Ronnie in the crowd. Terry was with Search and Rescue again today, having hardly slept since Tuesday. Kevin hadn't fared much better since his nephew disappeared, but he knew that what little sleep they'd had far exceeded hers. He would need to be sensitive. Ronnie was touchy on the best of days but the stress of the week had made her fragile, maybe unpredictable. His own daughter had been missing no more than a few hours and he was already on edge.

"If it were a kidnapper, he wouldn't be hiding in someone's home. Who would hide him? He'd have left after . . . taking Jimmy, but I don't think that's what happened."

"Then why haven't we found him yet?" his sister snapped. "It has to be someone in town!"

"We can't think that, Ronnie. We have to believe we'll find him. Search and Rescue hasn't stopped working since they got here. And Roseli—she . . . she just wandered off and she needs our help now, too."

"I'm tellin' ya, you can't ignore the houses." Several voices shouted affirmation.

"Forget it, Walt. Even if that was an option, it's not up to us. Sergeant Gilford will take care of that, if—"

"You really—"

"Walt!" Kevin bellowed. "Back off! We're trying to find my daughter—*your* granddaughter—and you're wasting time. You here to help?"

Surprise lit Blackwell's face, his pause reverberating in the cold air. Then he mumbled something and slid back behind a cluster of faces.

Kevin masked his own surprise as he stared his father-in-law down. He'd grumped at Walt before, but never in public. And Walt had never backed off. Awkward silence draped over the crowd before Kevin continued. "Okay, then. Let's save the postulating for later. Right now, we need to cover ground."

He laid out his plan with quick precision. The RCMP had already posted officers at the three roads leaving town. Kevin flanked the river with search parties travelling north and south along the bank from where they now stood. Four more teams would scour the streets, dragging their invisible net northward through yards instead of roaming the streets. Two groups would start in the center of town working outward, with two more working in from the fringes. The remaining few would hold court at strategic intersections near the corners of town with binoculars, allowing them to see if Roseli crossed the outer boundaries of the grid.

"I like it." Thomas pointed northeast. "Why don't we also have a group start at Willems Road by 200 and work back along the riverbank to meet up—"

Kevin shook his head. "We already have the advantage of having officers block that exit. They'll see if she comes along."

"Sure, but they're not mobile. We can close in a little faster this way. I can even take that group myself."

Kevin sighed. "I don't want to spend any more time on this. I've thought this through. We have people checking the river from here outward. We just need to get started."

"Look, I know you've got a lot on your mind right now, but that river—"

"He's right, Kevin," Walt said. "River's more dangerous than anything in town. If anything takes her, it'll be that. Another group out there would be the better choice. 'Sides, if you keep folks at the street corners, you won't need all the groups in town right away. If she's in town, she'll be a lot safer there before we find her."

Kevin's eyes sagged as he digested his father-in-law's words. Then he spoke, his voice hollow. "All right. Go."

The crowd faded into groups of four and set out for their posts, oblivious to the darkness settling into Kevin's clouded eyes.

∞ ∞ ∞

Kevin had formed the groups, but Blackwell made sure Wes Slater was with him. He needed somebody on his side after his son-in-law's outburst. *Damn that man!* He was a *good* man (Walt couldn't deny his daughter chose well, even if Kevin's city-soft core bothered him some), and Walt liked to see an edge in a man when things mattered, but that brief taste of public humiliation stuck like hot coal in his craw.

Murderous images flashed through his mind: pulping Kevin blow by blow in the town square, dragging him through the streets behind his too-shiny Jeep, hanging him by his heels from the bridge over the river. Small comforts Walt knew could never be, but comforts all the same.

He adjusted his binoculars to maximum range as he scanned the open field in the neighbouring country. Blackwell stood on the town's south dike, ninety feet from the invisible border. Autumn's wilt had begun, but waves of grass still stood tall enough to conceal most of a six-year-old girl. The grass rippled out for miles, trembling from the whisper of gentle wind.

The others in his group had fanned out and begun walking to the center of town, marching through yards one block at a time. Walt stayed back to peruse the field, being the lone searcher with long-range vision. In all his years in Argon, no child had broken the international border to wander through the fields. Everyone, it seemed, learned from birth that the field was off limits, due in no small part to the highway that split the town from such undiscovered country.

All the same, Walt figured, it was worth a look. If Roseli didn't turn up during the sweep, he would lead a group of four-wheelers out there himself, international border or no. Fortunately, the nights weren't cold enough to kill yet, but the longer she was gone . . . he grimaced at the thought of the Richmond boy as he swivelled his head eastward.

East of the prairie grass, he scouted the bordering ghost town for signs of life before doubling back across the field. Still nothing, but that only guaranteed she wasn't on her feet. He pushed aside the gloomy implication and let the scope dangle from his neck as he set off to join the rest of his party, still fuming at having been shown up in front of them.

In front of them, in front of dozens, in front of men like Stanley Gnocci.

Of all the things that Blackwell knew, three truths stood out in this moment like Georgie's neon sign at midnight (CHINESE and CANADIAN CUISINE, it crowed, as though the two went together like maple and bacon; not that Georgie served much syrup *or* bacon— his most popular "Canadian" item was not-really-Canadian Kraft Dinner, a delight for young children who still feared Americanized not-really-Chinese food): Blackwell knew he was a fixture in Argon, he knew *people* knew it, but he also knew that men like him needed men like Gnocci to make hay in politics. He wasn't in close with Gnocci, but had cultivated enough of a business relationship with him to ask for support when the time was right. Walt had been careful around Gnocci not out of any personal affection, but from the conventional wisdom of getting in with the richest man in the municipality. If he were to have any chance of building toward the mayor's seat, he would need to harness Gnocci's credibility, and he couldn't do that if he lost his own.

Blackwell typically bit back and relished antagonizing the local thorns in his pride, but he would have to play this one differently. A necessary evil, not strictly because Kevin was family but because of the timing. A public feud with his son-in-law in a time of distress? The optics would be less than mayoral.

Biting his tongue on this one would be the lesser humiliation, as long as folks were smart enough to see he was doing it for his grand-daughter's sake. But it still bothered him. Holding back felt too much like brown nosing. Blackwell was against brown nosing as a rule, but hell, there was a time for everything.

There was even a time to commend Thomas Larsen, he realized as he thought back to Larsen's contribution to Kevin's search plan. Adding the extra riverbank team was not only a nice gesture, but a smart idea. Then again, he never had Larsen pegged as an idiot. Quite the contrary, which was why the man had gotten on his nerves. But Larsen had befriended Kevin in a single summer and he showed up to help today. That was worth more than the hopers that hid indoors, more than the churchers that sat for their prayer sessions. They weren't all that way, but the ones who were might as well have turned their backs; ignoring reality and avoiding the real work—just another group of useless Christians with more faith than action.

On this day, at least, Walt couldn't deny that Larsen was a better man than some folks he'd known for years.

He hadn't seen that coming.

∞ ∞ ∞

The Red babbled loudly over the awkward silence of Thomas's designated search team as he led them along the bank, opposite the northward flow of the muddy river. The ache in his heart for Roseli overpowered all but the image of Mellie's expression when he left her at home with their daughter.

When Wade Slater had turned off Park Street onto the long, dirt Larsen driveway (yelling "She's sick, she's sick!" at the top of his lungs), Thomas hardly heard the chortle of the quad's engine over his wife's soft gasp as her garden-gloved hand went up to her mouth. They both dropped their rakes and ran over to see Bec, who was pale and sweaty but strong enough still to cling to the older boy.

Strong enough, indeed. Mellie pried gently at Bec's fingers to free Wade from her grasp, then lifted the girl up into her arms and squeezed. Thomas spoke with Wade and saw the boy off before leaving Bec with Mellie to help Kevin with the search effort.

As he left, Thomas exchanged a glance with Mellie that seared him. In it were the memories of two years of running, two years of moving from city to city to town, two years of fear that she had pushed beneath the surface but was now bubbling up from the depths of her soul. A part of her eyes still trusted him, but with a trust like an old quilt formed by squares of rich history: strong even now because of its foundation, but plagued with faded patches, frayed corners, and—more noticeable now than ever—a thread unravelling from corner to core.

And Thomas didn't know what to do.

Mellie was worried about her daughter, of course. That much was clear. But for him, worrying about Bec meant more than worrying about her well-being, it meant worrying about the well-being of *others,* too. Bec was so much like him (they'd seen enough of those signs in two years) and when he lost control, people got hurt.

Thomas had brought his family to Argon for a quiet life, which included teaching Bec to overcome the part of him he saw in her and wished away. He had come here to help her, but now Bec was hurt and her best friend was missing. He saw *that* in Mellie's eyes, too.

ARGON

But he hadn't come here to give up. Life in Argon had been good (minus Blackwell) their first few months, and long-term good practically *required* obstacles. Hadn't he once told Robbie you can't truly appreciate life until it hits back?

In the end, this would pass. Bec would recover. The ill-founded suspicion settling over their family would fade; he and Robbie hadn't taken Jimmy. Although Thomas didn't like what the missing kids meant, he was no kidnapper. Blackwell had been stirring that empty pot since the night Jimmy disappeared, and it wouldn't be long before everyone peered over the rim to find that this particular emperor had no stew.

∞ ∞ ∞

Kevin ignored the clawing branches as he stalked through the riverside forest, his group of five spread out fifteen feet from one to the next. Trent and Robbie flanked him while Bovarski and Ragnarsson worked the forest edges, searching for any sign of his daughter along the way.

He was hardly aware of the others. His mind recycled what Thomas had said at the rally point. Was his judgment really compromised? He couldn't be faulted for being stressed—his daughter was *missing.* Susanna was hysterical within minutes of learning that Roseli was gone. Ronnie was becoming rapidly more unstable, having gone four nights without her son. How much could any of them take if they couldn't find their children?

Kevin couldn't deny the dark fear growing like cancerous lesions in his mind, but even if his perception was failing, he was still the man with the most at stake in this particular search. That gave him the right to call the shots. Thomas probably hadn't given Jimmy

Richmond a second thought outside of search times. He'd only been here four months. Hardly enough time to care.

Kevin chided himself. Four months wasn't enough time to really know a man, but his gut had told him Thomas was trustworthy. Now his gut was silent and his head was swimming. Was he really losing his grasp? Or was Thomas turning against him?

His flanks abandoned him with steady determination as his thoughts lagged him. He swatted another attacking branch, but not before its tip scored a jagged line across his temple. He touched the pain and his finger came back red.

What stunned him more was that his father-in-law had backed down so quickly during their confrontation. That was not the Walt Blackwell he or anyone knew. Kevin could count the times that Walt had conceded an argument without using a finger. That man had drawn more blood with his tongue than the ruthless brambles ever would.

The gap between the searchers widened.

Kevin bristled as he thought of Walt siding with Thomas. Did Walt really think he wouldn't have covered all the bases? This was his *daughter* he was looking for! But maybe Walt was just being Walt, picking an argument in a bid for control. Would he do that now, in a time like this?

"Of course he would," Kevin said to the pine needle carpet around him. Why wouldn't he? But why back down, then? What had Walt seen in Kevin's eyes to curb his nature and quiet his tongue? Simple anger? Fear? *Instability?*

Kevin fought to push aside his growing suspicion. Probably just the stress and fatigue, aging him a decade in the past two hours.

A shout ahead drew his eyes into focus, revealing Bovarski waving something bright above his head. While drawing closer, Kevin ducked another branch, dodged an old stump, and skirted a small pit of birch root strands poking up through fresh, dark soil.

Kevin noticed Bovarksi's lips moving, Trent's wet eyes, and Robbie's thick look of disbelief. Kevin's eyes burned with recognition of the sun-coloured object that Bovarski thrust into his hand: the yellow rubber boot that he was now fixating on, with the pretty pink flower just below its lip, and—revealed as he turned the boot in his palm—the undeniable kindergarten scrawl in bold Sharpie on the dirty white underbelly. Just a single word, but the clearest she had so far learned to write:

Roseli

Kevin suppressed the nausea in his core and slowly rotated in place, scanning for small prints or broken branches, something that would lead him to his daughter. He looked down the slope by the river where he'd already been, hoping for an overlooked clue, following the spiderweb cracks along the dry riverbank. He looked through the trees up to the dike that bordered the forest a hundred feet away. Roseli might have navigated the thick forest, but she would have had to wander through someone's yard first to cross the dike.

Kevin raced through the trees, a dog on scent. Eyes wide and legs heavy, oblivious to the others trailing behind, he barrelled through branches as he scaled the dike. The first blur of house he saw from the top sent him reeling. He knew this back yard. He had visited it only weeks ago. He recalled recommending a fence at the time to his newest friend—"a must-have for everyone with kids and a home by the river," he had said. "The dike will keep the water out, but it won't keep the kids in."

The old home once had a fence protecting children from their curiosity, but the children were a distant memory when the fence heaved its final sigh years ago. Susanna's grandmother was too weak to host her grandkids, so she decided not to build another. No kids, no need. But it wasn't the old woman that had Kevin seething as he clutched the pretty little boot that was missing its girl. For this was not Stella Regent Blackwell's grand family home any longer. Not since she had given it up with the ghost nearly two years before.

The home belonged to Thomas and Mellie Larsen.

EIGHT

"Kevin found something! By the Larsens! Back past the dike!"
   "What is it?"
"Bovarski didn't say. Let's go!"

"Yeah, it was in the dirt. They found it behind his house!"
"Buried?"
"I don't know . . . oh my—"
"God help him if he took those kids. Ain't no one else'll keep
Terry from killing him if Jimmy's dead."

"Shouldn't we call Gilford?"
"The cops are watchin' the exits. Let 'em be."
"And slow down, let's not get carried away. What did they actually
find?"
"They found . . . I don't know, they found *something*. 'S it really
matter what it was?"

"Didn't Search and Rescue already sweep riverside?"

"That was two days ago. Roseli went missing *today*. He could have buried her *today!*"

∞ ∞ ∞

The stretch of forest behind the Larsen home buzzed with scores of curious citizens. As the searchers had marched through town toward the scene of Kevin's discovery, dozens poured from their yards and homes to join the procession. A little mystery went a long way in the typically tranquil town.

They wandered along the water's edge, tramped the forest growth, stared at ripples, tried to look helpful. A few worked spades or shovels, scouring freshly turned earth for telltale signs of burial. The slow herd shuffled along, pinballing from shoreline to tree line with accidental coordination.

Kevin kept his distance from Thomas while the search intensified. Roseli's boot had rattled him. She could have lost it honestly, but the whispers he'd been ignoring all week grew louder in his mind; in probably all of their minds. Where had Thomas come from? Some vague Wisconsin town Kevin never heard of, and had left it at that. What did he really know of Thomas? Was it merely coincidence that Roseli's boot was found directly behind the Larsen home?

Kevin heard shouts ahead. Someone had found something!

He raced along the bank, darting around searchers and straining against wind to hear the chatter. He couldn't make out words, just emotion; unbridled anger giving way to a crescendo of desperation. The forlorn image of his daughter's tiny body washing ashore flashed through his mind.

When he reached the clearing, the eye of the storm amidst an explosion of people, no body greeted him. Kevin exhaled. Thomas

ARGON

Larsen stood a few feet away with his shoulders slumped and face tight. His hollow eyes smoldered with fear and rage and resignation.

Ronnie was on her knees in the dry brown clay, head buried in her hands, moaning. Words slipped through her fingers as unintelligible shrieks that buckled under the weight of her anguished sobs. Then she lifted her head.

"It was *you!*" she screamed at Thomas over and over. "Tell me where my baby is!"

Kevin stood, transfixed by her screams. He couldn't blame her. Thomas wasn't giving them much reason to trust him. If he had taken Roseli, he might have noticed that she had lost her boot along the way. He could have suggested leading the riverside search so he could sweep behind his home without suspicion. But Kevin had reached it first.

Ronnie collapsed again. The crowd watched, waiting in silence for someone to make the first move. Thomas stared hard before finally turning and melting into the crowd.

Kevin crouched beside Ronnie and whispered her name. "We won't stop," he told her, "we'll look as long as it takes. But for now, go home and sleep, Veronica.

"Better yet, go home and pray."

NINE

Sunday brought fervent revival to the seven churches in Argon, at least for one morning. Ministers had already penned their prayers for Jimmy Richmond, who hadn't been seen since Tuesday, but Roseli's vanishment elevated the Argonian atmosphere from concern for one missing boy to an alarming fear that no child was safe.

The small church lots filled up with those who came to pray for the missing or try to make sense of the week's events. You could walk anywhere in Argon in no time at all, but for some of the most senior citizens, the short Sunday drive remained a weekly treat. Even the biggest of temples in the tiny town was cramped from the gaggle of sometime attenders and emotional infidels searching for salve: a brief respite from the despair of a fruitless search. Of the roll of eight hundred citizens, only the most religious atheists in Argon remained in their homes on this morning.

The Lutheran, United, and Anglican sanctuaries hummed with pre-service conversation, hushed though it was. The microscopic Orthodox Catholic tripled attendance from seventeen to standing room only. The first Baptist church in Argon—one hundred twelve years strong—flirted with full pews for the first time in its history. The First Baptist Church of Argon—the youngest of the town's churches at twenty-three years—was the biggest magnet of all, ballooning up to the balcony and back to the overflow room. Everyone knew which church the Richmonds and Grinbergs attended, and most had heard about what happened behind the Larsen home the day before.

Not one adult spoke as they waited for the service to begin.

Pastor Fricks started by acknowledging the week's events and the grief of the families waiting for their children to come home. The singing was muted, even among the regulars who knew all the words. When the final song faded, the pastor took his place at the dilapidated pulpit to address the somber crowd.

"I know it's been a while since we've done this, but before I pray, I want to open the floor to those of you who want to join in this morning. This has been an emotional week . . . a very difficult week for some of our families, and I know they will appreciate our continued support."

Old Mrs. Dyck started the session, to no one's surprise. She was a fixture not only at First Baptist but in Argon, having lived her eighty-two years within a ten-mile radius of town (with not a single trip to the big city, and none further than her second son's farm). It was a north-only radius, as she had never set foot in the United States, just a few feet from town limits. "Damn Americans and their guns," she'd say to all who'd listen. That refrain had aged with her, but when the town sweetheart prayed, they all knew that God was listening. Old Mrs. Dyck hadn't gone far, but her prayers had travelled the globe many times over, beseeching God's hand to move in every situation. Whenever she prayed, even the children in the chapel fell silent—a miracle in itself.

Two others followed suit before a pause. Fricks glanced over the congregation, gauging when to close the session with a prayer of his own. Time had taught him that public pray-ers ran a delicate racket: some could always be counted on to contribute from the heart, or duty, or narcissism. Others would join if the right prayers hadn't been delivered by the first pause. Then there were those who ached to add their part but struggled to overcome the anxiety of voicing it publicly. What those prayers lacked in clarity, they usually made up for in emotional impact.

So he waited. A few ticks, only, but an eternity long enough for the conflicted to win or lose the battle. On this day, he would later muse, he waited a moment too long.

His eyelids were closed, his mouth cracking open, when an unmistakable voice raw with emotion broke the silence.

"Oh God!" Veronica Richmond exclaimed, audibly trembling. Then she paused so long Fricks considered starting his own prayer before opening his eyes to see if she had fainted.

"Oh God," she repeated amid ragged gasps, "what . . . what is happening?" Standing alone atop the riser, Fricks sensed the temperature drop like desert nightfall as dozens of parishioners tensed. These were the folk who believed in standards, in process, in formulaic prayer; as though God needed guidance to determine what the person was trying to say. In truth, they were afraid of what the prayer might vocalize, afraid that the request might be too large, too disprovable. Fricks despised their tension, but mostly because he tensed, too. *Keep it safe,* he thought, *keep it vague, keep it rolling.*

"Please help," she continued, voice breaking, "where is . . . where is Jimmy? I know . . . I know you're in control . . . will you please bring him back? Will you please . . . please show us where he is? Show us . . . where they're keeping him?"

A low murmur rippled through the congregation.

"How could . . . why do . . ." Veronica stuttered through her sobs as Fricks contemplated divine interruption. "How could someone do this, God? Please bring Jimmy back and show those bastards for who they are!"

A smatter of shock escaped several lips, but the more hardened church-goers knew better than to make a scene. Ignore the cause, kill the problem.

Fricks leaped in with a prayer no one heard, an acknowledgment of human emotion, a reminder of God's power, a plea for guidance. The sermon that followed was electric in his mind, a desperate attempt to fade Veronica's Prayer from their collective memory. But even he could think of little else after the benediction.

∞ ∞ ∞

Congregants skipped the usual milling about after the service, opting instead to gather coats and kids and avoid awkward encounters. Mellie Larsen led the charge, stopping for no one and saving her tears until she closed her car door.

"I *told* you that going this morning was a bad idea!" she hissed at Thomas.

"Mellie, we can't let Ronnie dictate what we do! If we skipped this morning, she'd have convinced everyone that it's because we're guilty. If we're going to stay he—"

"We can't *stay!* Do you really think this is still going to work? Did you see what happened in there? No one—*no one*—stood up for us! Not even Kevin and Susanna!"

Why would they? he wanted to say. *How could they, in that environment? Ronnie was overreacting. Surely everyone could see that.*

Thomas backed out of the parking stall with a careful turn of the family car, an '88 Chevy Caprice wagon (beige with faux wood panels and a fold-down rear-facing back seat; a classic in theory only but reliable enough to keep ticking nearly thirty years and two transmissions later). He guided the car through a parade of parishioners, ignoring the stares raining down like a torrent of brimstone. "I'm sorry. I thought . . . I really thought that yesterday was just . . . some drama that she needed to get out of her system."

"Drama? She accused us of taking her child—in a public prayer!"

"Her boy's been missing almost a week."

"She's going to turn everyone against us! Why are you taking her side?"

"I'm not taking her side, Mellie, but we can't turn on her just because she's not thinking clearly. If we want people to believe us, we can't start slinging back. One person chooses to believe the gossip and it's all downhill from there."

"Stop defending her, Thomas! She's unstable! And the worst of it is, everybody knows her," she said as her voice broke, "everybody listens to her."

Thomas shook his head. "No one will believe her. Not that."

"They already do, Thomas. Don't be so ignorant." Mellie looked at him, fear and anger shadowing her face. "We have to get away from this town."

TEN

Robbie tossed and turned for hours Sunday night. He couldn't get Jimmy out of his mind, and whatever it was that devoured him. Now Roseli was missing, but Robbie was confused. Had she been taken from behind his own house? Could the killer slide (or whatever was in it) have moved? Roseli's boot had been far from the playground.

Clouds covered the moon. All that crept through the window tonight was darkness, but for a fringe glow from the street lamp at the end of the driveway.

Every time he closed his eyes, Robbie saw only the hole, the mouth—the portal?—that had taken his friend. Jimmy's unsuspecting face laughed again and again as he left the red plastic runway behind and vanished into nothingness.

Where had he gone? Robbie's mind raced with possibilities: Had he really been eaten? Sent into darkness? Gone to the weeping and gnashing of teeth?

Robbie felt compelled to get on his knees and reach for the heavens, then wondered if what took Jimmy might be waiting under his bed.

He pulled the covers tighter.

Through the thin fabric over his open eyes, he noticed a flicker, then more on its heels; erratic bits of light flashed outside his window. The heavy breathing that had filled his ears since drawing the covers up disappeared. He imagined the bits of light twinkling along the slide before it opened its jaws for Jimmy, and twinkling in the air before taking Roseli away forever. Were the lights now coming for him?

With breath abated, Robbie tugged the blanket down. Past his hair. Past his forehead.

Past his eyes.

His room sat still, black, waiting. Robbie didn't dare peer over the edge of his bed. He stared at the ceiling instead, shooing his fear away.

The flickers returned, streaking past his window like tiny comets burning bright and fading fast. Robbie sat up in his bed just enough to reach the window. Before this week, he had loved the window. Before Argon, he had never enjoyed such a view. From his vantage point two-and-a-half storeys up, he could see through the breaks in the tall trees at the end of his driveway to the school and beyond. Any time the action started in the ball field or at the playground, he was a brief jaunt from joining.

He hadn't liked the view much this week. All he thought about when he stared out the window was Jimmy, dead and gone.

Or maybe worse, just gone.

Robbie checked over his shoulder to the dark corners of his bedroom, then set his gaze outdoors. Down past the end of the long driveway, an obscured figure scurried toward the path on the far side of Park Street, flashlight jostling. Robbie's eyes grew wide as the figure took the path between the houses and blinked away into the night.

It was headed for the playground.

ARGON

Robbie forgot about the thing that might be under his bed and tiptoed out of his room. Down the hall, away from Bec's bedroom, past his parents' door. He took great care to avoid the squeakiest parts of the floor he had discovered during a few other late-night escapes in summer. He tugged his jacket and runners on and opened the door (unlocked, but no surprise there—the family had stopped locking it their third week in town—although Robbie *had* noticed Mom locking it most nights this week).

He grabbed his Easton maple from the front yard with both hands and gave it a test swing. He couldn't hit the ball as far with it yet as with his old aluminum bat, but he'd fallen in love with the texture the first time he picked it up.

Robbie looked both ways as he approached the street, but only to make sure no one else was around to see him. He darted across, wielding the bat like a sword as he skulked along the dark path. He hadn't brought a flashlight—couldn't risk being seen—but every tree branch seemed to lunge for him as he passed beneath their scraggly claws.

The path opened to the school field and Robbie felt suddenly vulnerable. He dropped to all fours and pressed low to the damp ground. Blades of grass brushed his cheeks as he scampered like a wounded spider, clumping ahead with bat in hand.

Then he was there. He sensed the playground before he saw it, feeling its presence in the darkness like a spectre's frosty breath on his neck. Not a light dotted the night; the skulking figure had turned off the flashlight (or bypassed the playground altogether, and Robbie was chasing shadows).

Robbie wriggled to the wooden boundary surrounding the playground. Peering over the log, he could see only part of the slide where Jimmy had disappeared. As he squinted through the darkness, he imagined where else the hungry portal might have struck:

Hovering at the foot of the monkey bars, ready to swallow up kids as they dropped to the platform.

Waiting beside the merry-go-round, snatching rogue children who hung wildly from the ride.

Camping out at the base of the fire pole, where unsuspecting sliders would twirl into oblivion.

After convincing himself that he was alone, Robbie swung a foot over the wooden beam and stepped onto the sand. Now that he was here, he wanted a closer look at the slide. Daylight hadn't revealed any clues, but what if the threat hadn't been there during the day? Maybe it *had* moved . . . lying low in the woods, waiting for someone like Roseli to come alone.

Then again, if it *was* back, why on earth was he walking toward it instead of running away?

Clutching the bat with a hitter's poise, he inched forward. Sand crunched under his soles as he reached the monkey bars, passed beneath the gymnastic rings, and moved toward the twisty slide, its exit hidden from view behind the bottom curl.

Jimmy spun through Robbie's mind again as he approached, but disappeared with the sound of sand shuffling on the other side of the slide. Robbie froze and raised the bat above his head.

Something was there. Waiting.

As Robbie contemplated whether to swing, the world slowed to a crawl around him. His hearing sharpened as if drawing power from his other senses: though his eyes had begun to adjust to the darkness, the night blurred before him; the sweet night air faded from his nose; his tongue dried to chalk and the bat became like heavy stone in his hands.

From around the slide, Robbie heard the cautious breathing of one attempting to keep quiet. Whatever was there had heard him.

Whatever was there had opted not to speak, not to signal that he was a friend. Robbie dug his heels into the sand.

A burst of light flared around the edge of the slide, blinding Robbie. His perfect hearing died, replaced by a dull hum. Propelled by instinct, he stepped forward and swung.

Maple struck metal and his bat kept going. *Follow through, Rob. Turn those singles into doubles.* His dad's voice rang clear in his mind from summer practice. *Extra bases win ball games.* A loud cracking sound split the calm as the bat found plastic. Follow through, indeed. Dad would have been proud.

"Robbie!"

The voice was unmistakable. Robbie looked in its direction, blinking the dancing spots away. The blinding light was gone now—he suspected the metal *thwack* had reported the death of a flashlight—but even in the darkness, he knew who stood just inches away.

His dad.

"What are you doing here?"

Robbie was too busy finding his breath to answer. He clutched the bat, still gasping.

"Why aren't you in bed?"

"I . . . couldn't sleep. Saw the flashlight."

"And you thought . . ."

"I—I don't know what I thought. I saw the light and where it was headed, and I had to see what was going on."

His dad was just visible enough now for Robbie to see his head shaking. "With your bat."

Robbie set the barrel down and braced himself on the knob. The spots were fading but his head still swam, and his knees bobbed like a teapot in a tempest. "What are *you* doing here?"

"Things have been getting hairy this week, as you know." His father's shadowy face stared down at him. "A lot of attention coming our way. I've been looking for something that can point it elsewhere."

"Why here?"

"Jimmy's dad said this was the last place he was, far as he knows. But I've been out back of the house, behind the dike this evening, too. I had to be careful with that, and wait until everyone turned in so they wouldn't see me cross the dike."

"Did you find anything?"

"Nothing there. Here, just a home run hitter and a broken flashlight."

Robbie grimaced. "Sorry."

"Can't really blame you. I can imagine what was going through your mind. I turned the light off when I reached the field because I didn't want any sleepless neighbours seeing me out here this late. Wouldn't build much confidence, would it?"

Nausea swept through Robbie, wringing cold sweat from every pore.

"You sure did a number on the slide."

Robbie didn't look. An acrid storm was marching through his stomach.

"We'll have to talk to the school about that, son." His dad's tone sharpened. "Are you listening?"

Robbie dropped to his knees and gripped the bat with both hands. The storm billowed up through his chest and arms like a cauldron overflowing, stopping his breath and melting the nerves in his arms. He opened his mouth to set it all free, but nothing came but a moan. Then he was on his back, waking. Somewhere distant, the stars grew hands and reached down from the heavens to shake his shoulders and call his name.

The earth was soft and hard and lumpy beneath him. Cold crystals clung to the back of his neck. He had *only* a neck for a moment until feeling returned to his body in patches, as though a master controller slid levers from off to on in slow-motion madness. Toes, up. Knees, on line. Arms and elbows, good to go.

A sound like his name reached him again, so he tried to reply but spoke only garble.

His father stood in full view now with stars like fireflies around him, his lips moving, speaking his own brand of garble to Robbie until the sounds formed slowly into something resembling words: up, okay, hegg. Head.

Robbie sat up. "I'm . . . okay. What happened?"

"You fainted."

"I felt sick. It's . . . mostly gone. Mostly."

His father nodded. "You were running on adrenaline there, Rob. When it levelled off, I think your body just realized how tired it was. Chasing monsters in the dark can get pretty tense. But everything's okay now."

Robbie shivered as the sand turned to ice beneath him. The cool air pricked his throat as he sucked it in. He looked up in the darkness, but instead of his father he saw only Jimmy vanishing over and over again in an infinite loop of his own making. He could hold the haunting truth no longer. He searched for his father's face.

"No . . . no, Dad, it's not. Not okay." Tears rolled down his cheeks like beads of guilt in search of atonement. "It's my fault. I should have said something. Jimmy . . . and now Roseli's gone and it's because of me!"

Thomas knelt closer. "What do you mean?"

"We were playing . . . on Tuesday, five of us. We came back here from the river because it was almost supper time. We were just playing. We were playing Twisties and I was 'It' and I was chasing him—

chasing Jimmy—and he slid down the slide and I was waiting at the bottom and . . . and I told him he's *dead* and then . . . and he just— the slide curled up at the bottom and ate him!" Guttural sobs racked him. "And now Roseli's gone because I, I wished it on her when Bec didn't come back for chores yesterday. It was me! And everybody thinks it's you."

Thomas wrapped his arms around his son, eyes wide. He held tight as Robbie cried and shuddered, and didn't say a word until the boy stopped shaking. "Robbie, who was there with you on Tuesday?"

Robbie drew a breath that didn't sting quite so much anymore. "There was me and Trent and Alfie, and—"

"Was your sister there?"

"What?"

"Your sister. Was she with you?"

"No. Well, she wasn't playing with us. She was over with Maddy and Roseli. On the swings, I think."

Thomas wrung his hands and looked away, muttering softly.

"What is it?"

"Oh, Robbie," Thomas said, his face weary, "there's something you need to hear."

ELEVEN

Thomas sat in the sand across from his son, a bleak smile aging his face in the night. This was a conversation he had played out often in his mind, but now that its time had come, his polished script crumbled like a dusty, yellowed map that marked no place to go.

"Robbie, our family has . . . a unique history. What I'm about to tell you cannot be repeated. Except for your own kids one day, it's very important that you share this with nobody—no one—*ever*."

A cloud shifted, revealing Robbie's frown in the light of the intermittent moon.

"The first thing you need to know is that this is not your fault. What happened to Jimmy had nothing to do with you. I've suspected since we searched that first night that Jimmy wasn't taken by anyone." His gaze dropped. "I almost wish he had been." Thomas looked back to his son. "But it wasn't you.

"For centuries, some in our family have been . . . granted a connection of sorts, to nature. A link to their environment that, that . . . an ability to affect what's around us, b—"

"You mean with our minds?"

"Maybe. Well, yes, in a way, but this isn't strictly some ability of the mind."

"Then what is it?"

"With psychokinesis—mind control, basically—the person controls what's around them. But with this ability, we can't control what happens. The best we can do is try to keep it from happening in the first place. That's not easy, because it feeds off of fear. Off any emotions, really, but fear tends to be the strongest. That fear opens up the . . . it activates the ability, and takes away the problem."

"Problem?" Robbie's voice caught in his throat and he swallowed hard. "Jimmy wasn't a *problem!*"

"It doesn't know that, son. It's not intelligent, it's reactive. It's a response of our emotion, not a being or, or a decision. For all I know about it, I still don't know what it really is or why it affects us. No one in the family figured out a way to stop it yet—the best any of us have done is suppress it—but it isn't here to be figured out. It's just *here*. It's a disease, I suppose, and we're carriers. This is why you can never say anything about this—and trust me, I know how difficult that will be. If it were psychokinesis, telekinesis, clairvoyance . . . that still sounds sketchy, but it's a *known* unknown. It's on people's radar to a degree. They'll believe it or they won't; they'll respect us or ridicule us, and we can live with that. But if they learn what really happens—what this ability really is—it'll frighten them, Robbie, because it's completely foreign." He pierced his son's eyes with a grim stare. "Good people do ugly things to each other when they're scared."

"What do you mean?"

Thomas sighed. He didn't want to frighten his son further, but he couldn't stop now. He lowered his voice and began recounting the stories his mother had told him: a brutal, jarring account of Larsen history.

Erik Larsen, gutted by his neighbours after fending off an attacking party at the village shoreline. They owed him their survival but couldn't reconcile the image of an entire Viking ship swallowed up by the sea.

Torvald, a nomadic fugitive forced into the Egyptian army after fleeing south to escape execution. Along with sparking a family line throughout Europe, he compelled a desert sandstorm to devour an insuperable Persian army.

Marin, a saint who lived eleven years in a hollowed-out tree. A selfless act not for penance as the people thought, but to protect his community from the curse that raged within.

And Lili Larsen, burned at the stake as a suspected witch—"probably the closest Wurzburg ever was to being right". Family legend held that young Lili's fear so consumed her that a shock wave reduced most of the onlookers to ash, even as she breathed her last.

"Whatever it is, it's intent on eliminating the cause of the fear that activates it. Like it's trying to help, except it doesn't. Usually makes things worse."

Robbie traced circles in the sand. "So I can't ever stop it?"

"Oh. Robbie, no, you can't stop it. You don't even have it, son."

"What? But I was there, right next to Jimmy when it took him!"

"I don't know why, but you don't have this ability. Most don't; in fact, it seems to only show up once per generation, sometimes not at all. That's how I know this wasn't you."

Thomas paused, watching Robbie's quizzical look deepen until the answer finally ambushed him. "Bec!"

Thomas nodded. "Something must have frightened her, so she reacted. That's what took Jimmy away, not you. The ability seems to skip a generation here and there, but I haven't heard of it happening twice in a single generation. We all carry it—I'm pretty sure of that—

or it would have disappeared by now."

"How do you know so much about it?"

"Your grandma, mostly. She told me a lot about the family history when I was a boy. Wouldn't *stop* telling me, as though she was trying to rid herself of it by speaking it away. Once she was gone, my uncle taught me some of what he knew."

Robbie's eyes narrowed. "You have it, too!"

Thomas exhaled slowly, delaying the inevitable truth. "I do." He watched Robbie's eyes flash in the pale light of the moon: anger, fear, awe, jealousy.

"So they're right? It *is* you. Well, it's Bec, but you're just like her. And what about your mom?"

"I don't think so, no. I've wondered, though. She was here one day, gone the next. I've wondered if this ability did it to her—took her away—but that was just me trying to make sense of the pain. She didn't have it, my uncle had it. He taught me how to control it—bury it, really; complete control is an illusion. But I'll do my best to teach your sister the same thing: allow herself to fear without it consuming her or everyone around her."

"Can't you bring Jimmy back?" Robbie traced the sand with both hands. "I wish I had it. I could bring Jimmy back. Jimmy would still be here!"

Thomas shook his head. "Oh, Robbie, you don't want this."

"But you have it."

"Trust me, this is a curse, not something to wish for. Maybe even a real curse. My mother told me that her great-grandfather Franz believed that this was what the Bible refers to with the sins carrying to the fourth generation, at least for our family. He thought that if he could live his life without giving in to the power inside, the curse would end."

"Did it w—" Robbie cut himself off as logic caught up to his question. "It didn't work."

"No, not like he hoped. Not at all, obviously. And, as the story goes, one of his sons realized that ignoring it would do nothing, so he decided to explore the ability and find out what it could do."

"What happened?"

"I don't know, he disappeared. All my mother knew was a rumour that he worked on a research team during World War Two."

"Oh."

"With the Germans."

"Oh!" Robbie's face churned. "Was he a, a—"

"A Nazi? I guess he worked with them, but I don't know his loyalties. Your grandma was pretty adamant that he wasn't, but she never knew him. It might have just been wishful thinking on her part."

"What if he found out how to bring someone back?"

"That was a long time ago, Robbie. None of them are even alive anymore. I never knew him, or even my grandparents. I hardly knew my mother, and I don't want that for you and your sister. I'm trying to find a way to give you a normal life." He sighed. "Besides, the ability doesn't work like that. You can't dictate what happens. It's a reaction, not a conscious ability." Thomas placed his hands on Robbie's knees. "Son, this is hard, I know, but we have to think of Bec. She's not aware of what's happening; she doesn't even understand that this has anything to do with her. Your mom and I aren't sure if she's old enough yet for the discussion, but it's coming. Once she does know, I need to teach her how to control it, not explore it."

"But why would you let her play with Roseli, or with anyone? That's dangerous. What if she gets angry?"

"Yes." Thomas closed his eyes and scrunched his forehead. "You're right. Robbie, this is very difficult for your mom and me. But we've watched her since she started showing signs a few years ago, and the signs don't show up just because she gets angry. It's mostly when there's an element of shock involved, and not even then, not always.

"We don't want to hurt anyone, but we can't help your sister by locking her inside. Even if it happens again. I won't change our routine. If we start hiding ourselves away—or her—suspicion will only increase. And she needs the opportunity to face this herself if she's going to live with it."

Thomas placed a hand on his son's arm. "You see, Robbie, I think Franz was on the right track. We can beat this if we learn to control the triggers. With Bec, though, she's so young, so reactive. She's still learning how to respond in normal situations, let alone to this added burden—so hiding her away takes that chance away from her. Surrounding ourselves with the right people and finding a community that protects each other is critical to helping her control this."

"That's why we keep moving."

A history of regret etched its portrait across Thomas's brow. "Yes. *Kept* moving. I don't want to move anymore. The cities, the bigger towns, haven't worked. Too much can go wrong. But I don't know. Maybe it's not about how many people. Maybe people are just people, no matter where you go." His voice strained. "But it has to work somewhere. Why not Argon?"

"But Mom wants to leave, I can tell—"

"Bec is changing, developing more quickly than I expected. She'd been doing so well since we arrived here, wasn't showing any of the symptoms that forced us to move the other times." He fell silent as he contemplated how much to share with Robbie. "Those symptoms were nothing like this. Nothing this severe ever happened before. Not with her. But I can't deny that it *is* her. We just need to weather the storm and help her adapt—maybe . . ." he shook his head sadly, "I just wanted this to be the town that's . . . that's worthy of this *thing*."

"But you don't think telling Bec will help?"

"Frightening her won't help, not right now. With you . . . I can trust you to keep this to yourself, to keep our family safe. Bec isn't ready for that responsibility yet."

"We have to stay, Dad. I don't ever want to move again."

"Rob . . ."

"Where are they? Are they alive? Where did they go?"

"Robbie, I wish I—" The grass rustled behind them, and Thomas froze. He glanced back, then looked at Robbie and put a finger on his lips. He stood and moved slowly in the direction of the abrupt sound, but the sand and stone beneath his feet announced his movement. The rustling began again, this time moving steadily away from the playground and accompanied by the soft thud of footfalls.

Thomas cursed his flashlight for being broken and turned back to Robbie, mind racing. "Grab your bat. Let's go."

Robbie jumped up, bat in hand. "Who was it?"

"I don't know. We can only hope they weren't there for long." Even as he spoke, panic railed against him. He had spoken his son's name. The eavesdropper was sure to have heard that. He berated himself for being so careless, for thinking the late night was theirs alone. He should have taken Robbie home and told him there.

Thomas took Robbie's hand and led him home, hurrying through the dark field as the night breeze swirled around them.

TWELVE

Monday was hell for Robbie.

He spent the morning worrying that everyone would know the broken slide was his fault. Every look was an accusation. He reminded himself that they stared because they thought his dad was a kidnapper, but that didn't help.

After breakfast, his dad had whispered to him that the family didn't need "more negative attention" right now, so they would take responsibility for the slide anonymously. All Robbie had to do was slip an unmarked envelope—stuffed with cash and a hand-printed apology in block letters—under the principal's door when no one was looking. Of course, he still had some work ahead of him to pay back half of that cash to his dad.

When the students squawked during morning recess about having the slide roped off, he was sure they were all looking at him. Maddy gave him the evil eye (that was typical), but what bothered him more was the growing group of boys jabbing at him with fingers and eyes all around the schoolyard. Plotting under their collective breath.

Worse, he didn't have Trent to back him up. Trent joined his parents for Monday's search while the family tried to stay hopeful about finding Roseli. Fuelling that optimism: many other parents, including Robbie's own, decided to skip work and keep searching for the missing kids. (Robbie wanted to be out there helping, but his dad told him that the town needed stability just as much as searchers, and he wanted Robbie to help by getting things back to normal. Normal meant school.)

The glares grew colder from across the lunchroom.

The vultures swooped in during afternoon recess. The older boys stalked him, including him in their games but growing more violent as they played. They bumped and pushed and tripped him until they were all around the corner suddenly, behind the school, away from the teachers and the beefed-up recess duty team. Robbie had seen boys like this in other schools; somehow, they always found the blind spots.

They circled him. Wade, a year older than Robbie and sporting an early hair on his chin, led the charge.

"My dad says Jimmy and Roseli are prob'ly in your basement, freak." Robbie searched his human cage for a hole. Nothing. "He says we should string you up and search your house, *freak*." Wade two-handed Robbie's tee and shoved, and the younger boy stumbled back against Wade's cronies. "How ya like that, FREAK!"

The cronies knocked him to the ground as the school bell announced the end of recess. Wade swore and kicked Robbie. "Let's go," he muttered. "Teacher'll be coming any second."

Stares flew at him like horseflies swarming as the students filed inside. Back in class, paper pellets bit his neck and ears, flung from Sandeep's makeshift launcher. Sandeep hung with Jimmy and had been Robbie's friend until his parents joined the anti-Larsen bandwagon last week on account of moving up a rung on the new-family-in-town pecking order. The Larsens had more or less leapfrogged them over the summer until the children started disappearing.

Robbie heard the whispers mounting and saw the steady flow of notes exchange hands during final period, so he was hardly surprised when Sandeep bumped him on the way out of class and Wade slammed him in the hallway. Marcus joined in before Mrs. Allen warned them off, slowing them enough for Robbie to close his backpack and head to the bike rack. He wanted to rush off and leave his tormentors behind, but his sister joined him every day after school and he knew not showing up would frighten her. He didn't want to be responsible for how that fear might manifest. It wasn't fair to him, but he couldn't put his sister in that position.

Robbie unlocked his bike and fiddled with the worn handle grips. He was thinking of how good a new set of grips would look—nothing fancy, just with more cushion so his knuckles and elbows would stop rattling with every bump or jarring when he landed off Dead Man's Jump—when a hard shove sent him to the concrete and his bike skittering over with a loud crash. Pain swept like fire across his palms and up through his wrists, but he rose deliberately to face his attacker.

Wade and Marcus watched him stand as several other boys huddled around. Sandeep stood back, out of arm's reach. Robbie brushed off his hands, which were skinned and burning like flaming stubs of flesh at the end of his arms. He saw the blood dotting and pooling on his palms then looked up, kept lifting his eyes until they locked with Wade's.

"Where's the other boot, Larsen?" Wade spat his name like poison. No more Robbie, just Larsen. Just another of the vile clan.

A strange quiet settled over Robbie at the sound of his surname. This was different from the ridicule he had lived through in other towns. This was about more than simply being an outsider, an easy target. Genuine contempt spread through Wade's eyes, making him appear much older than his thirteen years. Much more dangerous.

Wade's lips kept twisting, forming new weapons as the others joined his verbal assault. Their faces grew darker as they shouted crude epithets. Their arms grew longer and pushed him away. They beat him back but moved ever closer, surrounding him with their wicked party, shouting, pushing, pulling, beating. He bounced from fist to fist, tasting hatred and fear but feeling nothing but tears burning rivulets along his nose down to his chin.

Then, from under the drooping willow where they had dragged him, he looked past the tree and saw Bec.

∞ ∞ ∞

Bec had exited the school and was headed for the bike rack, eyes bright. When she saw Robbie's bike prone in the dirt, she scanned the yard from the empty playground to the bare expanse of wind-swept sports fields to the willow where students had gathered like starving maggots to a rotting meal.

She ran for the crowd, then squirmed through the mass of writhing hips and knees until she saw the big boys with their bloodied knuckles and bruising words, smelling of rage and cowardice. She looked at their prey, saw her brother behind the purple face and red eyes, and gasped. And before the breath had passed her lips, the giant willow arched lower, grasped the boys who still held Robbie with its gnarled fingers and flung them into its trunk, into a mouth that vanished as quickly as it appeared.

The onlookers paused—in unison—for the length of a single heartbeat that would reverberate through the rest of their lives. The image seared their young minds like white-hot iron branding a

ARGON

collective scar, a memory of which most would never speak a word. There was no sense in it, even to those with worlds of imagination, but there was no denying that the tree had eaten Marcus and Patterson. The two boys had been holding Robbie one moment and been taken the next, leaving their victim staring up from the grass, more frightened by his saviour than he had been by the boys.

A chorus of screams exploded across the field as the children ran for their homes, strewing bikes and backpacks in their wake. Bec ran with them, leaving her brother behind.

Robbie watched them flee. "It wasn't me!" he shouted. "It was—" he stopped, eyes flaming, unable to speak her name. His sister had just uprooted him unwittingly from Argon. She was tearing him away from his friends, forcing the family to move. Again! Yet he had to protect her?

He ran to his bike, oblivious to the cuts on his face and the loll of his eyelid. He rode off, away from the screams, away from his home, away from the willow that now looked as safe and sad and lonely as it always had.

THIRTEEN

Kevin peered out the kitchen window. "What is he doing?" He swore and his wife brought her head up sharply.

"What's wrong?"

"Something's happening. Your idiot father's got everyone wild." Kevin was out the door before he'd pulled his jacket on the whole way.

Susanna walked to the kitchen and looked out the window into the street, eyes red from another bout of weeping during a break from the search. She couldn't see Walt, but did see the twenty-odd people rambling down the street, westward. Toward the Larsen's house, it appeared. Her father had done the unthinkable.

He'd stirred him up a mob.

∞ ∞ ∞

Even before Kevin caught up to his neighbours, he could sense the panic winding through the roving mass. Once he reached them, they bombarded him with varying reports of what occurred at the school.

Despite conflicting theories, it was evident that more kids were missing. Maybe a dozen. Children had come home screaming and in tears, and parents were still swapping story fragments as they rumbled forward, trying to find common threads.

Few were calm, but the parents whose children had not returned home were a special breed of frantic. They knew little, but they knew that *something had happened,* and their kids hadn't come home after school.

Robbie Larsen bubbled to the surface of every conversation. Many kids had fingered him by name, though Kevin couldn't decipher if Robbie was responsible for the latest disappearances or if he himself had disappeared.

Kevin shoved his way through the crowd of mostly friends to where Blackwell and Wes Slater swaggered ahead of the pack. "What's going on?"

"Time to put an end to this, Kevin," Blackwell replied, "Larsen can't get away with doing this anymore."

"What is 'this', exactly?"

"More of our kids are missing. Right from under our noses. Can't even tell yet how many this time."

"So you're going to storm his house?"

"I woulda thought you'd be all for it with Roseli gone."

Kevin envisioned his hands around his father-in-law's throat, crushing Blackwell's crude logic in mid-speech before more spilled out. "Stop this."

"We're jus' gonna talk to him."

"You can't—" he gestured to the flock at their heels. "You can't do it like this, Walt. This is chaos!"

Blackwell grinned. "Wasn't my idea, Kevin. Jus' came together. I'm just helpin'."

"Yeah. Sure you are."

"You don't like it, *you* try talkin' everybody down. Wes heard some inneresting news last night about that boy. Caught them whisp'rin' in the dark at the school playground, if that don't beat all. Larsen's got a secret, jus' like I told you."

"What secret?"

The way Walt smiled, Kevin half-expected to hear a canary warble its death song from the bottom of Blackwell's throat. "Don't know exactly, but Wes says he's hidin' *something.*"

Kevin slowed slightly, allowing the mob to absorb him again. Debating with Blackwell would be like lying down to block an avalanche. His time would be better spent petitioning his friends, even as they all rolled together down the street to Larsen's home.

∞ ∞ ∞

Walt Blackwell had never led a mob before this day, but that didn't stop him from relishing his impromptu role. Slater's report that morning of Larsen's secret meeting confirmed his longstanding suspicions, so when the grapevine told him more kids had disappeared, his gears were greased to lead the charge. He would find the kids, end the fear that had been infecting folks for the past week, and make sure young Larsen paid for whatever the hell he was doing.

Blackwell's adrenaline blazed as he scaled the stairs to the Larsen's front entrance. The door was probably unlocked, but he didn't touch the knob. Even if it was locked, he had a key back home, of course— he *was* the landlord—but this . . . this was a *Moment.* The kind of game changer that required a heavy dose of drama. Drama was what folks remembered, and when this was over, he would win the mayor's race in a landslide. With or without Gnocci's blasted seal of approval.

The power of the crowd behind electrified him as he pounded on the door like a devil on a war drum.

Thomas emerged from his garage with a wrench and a rag and surveyed the crowd. "What's going on, Walt?"

Blackwell jerked from the door like a deer feeling buckshot, then recovered and bellowed down, "Where's your boy, Larsen?"

Thomas polished the wrench with the grimy rag as he drew a long breath. "What business you have with Robbie?"

"Somethin' happened at the school." Blackwell lowered his voice, but not enough to cede control. "Two more boys are missing and the kids are all saying your boy did somethin'. Scared 'em half to hell."

Thomas peered through narrowed eyes. "What exactly happened?"

"Hard to know for sure. The kids aren't makin' much sense. There was a fight at the school, they're all scared and are talkin' monsters. And more kids are unaccounted for." Blackwell let the words settle. "Where's your boy?"

Thomas shook his head. The crowd parted as he worked his way toward the steps. "No. You want to talk to my son about this, that's fine. But you don't come to my door like this, Walt. With a crowd. He's just a boy." He scanned the group, features hardening. "I'll go in and get him. And if you want me to open this door again, why don't you pick two of you to talk to Robbie and the rest of you go home. You'll get your details later. You won't get any answers by scaring him." He closed the door quickly without slamming.

Neighbours exchanged glances. Kevin watched from the edge of the crowd for Blackwell's next move. Blackwell stared at the oak door long after the closing click, seething and thinking. Awkward silence devolved into the nervous shifting of pubescent students at a pre-teen dance. Blackwell let the tension escalate for a long moment before turning to face his anxious mob.

"One more minute," he instructed, his voice rising with every word, "and then we're going in."

Kevin blanched. His heart began to race, anticipating certain disaster. The pounding rose to his throat as he considered what to say. He had to say something. They all had to speak out, didn't they? But as he watched the pasty faces flush with rage or guilt or fear, he knew they would say nothing. Because he knew he should speak and yet *he* said nothing. Civility was a cause drowning in his desire to simply *find his daughter*. Each silent moment drained his fading urge to speak and sucked away his will to contend against the shifting, intangible evil rising up like Reduviidae among them.

"Don't forget the cellar."

Heads bobbed and whirled at the words. Susanna was walking up the long driveway of her grandmother's old home. "When I was a girl," she continued, "I'd spend hours playing here. In the house, in the yard, out behind by the dike. But the one place I never would go, the one place that scared me clear off, was the cellar. If the Larsens are taking our children," her eyes reddened as she cleared her throat, "seems like the place to start."

Eyes widened and mouths hung ajar as her implication settled across the crowd. Kevin stared at his wife, stunned. Everyone else looked to their impromptu leader (elected by a unanimous vote of feet following fear).

Blackwell waited, basking in their gaze as he watched a salty stream trickle to Susanna's chin. He knew the cellar, of course. He'd grown up in this home and had been sent on errand to the cellar many times as a youth. But he knew the cellar would produce nothing: he'd had no key to give to Larsen with the rental agreement—Stella Regent Blackwell had lost the key some years past and Walt had never gotten around to bringing his cutters.

But he also knew it would look good to his mob. A padlocked cellar door was key evidence in a case of speculation—besides, Larsen could have found the key by sheer luck or cut the lock and found his morgue.

Blackwell walked down to ground level and pushed through the crowd to reach his daughter. He wrapped a heavy arm around her shoulders, pulled her in, and planted a loud kiss on her forehead.

Then—tugging her forward in an awkward show of solidarity—he set out with Susanna toward the Blackwell cellar door.

FOURTEEN

"What do they want?"

Thomas secured the deadbolt and leaned back against the door. He contemplated telling his wife that everything was fine, it would all turn out okay, but he knew that her fear would not be extinguished by empty placation. "Robbie."

Mellie's face fell. "The fight?"

"What fight?"

"Bec was upset after school. She said the big boys were fighting Robbie."

"What happened?"

"He ran off. She said they *all* ran away."

Thomas frowned. "Walt said a lot of kids are missing."

"Missing? Thomas, Robbie's not here."

"I know."

"He didn't come home after school."

"I know." His brow darkened. "Mellie, I don't think they're concerned about the fight."

She peered through the split in the bay window curtain. "Why not?"

"Something Walt said. It isn't good."

"What did he say?"

"Some of the kids that saw what happened are saying that Robbie made the other boys disappear."

"What? That's impossible! Isn't it?"

"Yes. Well, probably, unless he's a late bloomer. But Bec was there, and she saw the fight. Makes sense."

Mellie laughed, a petrifying rasp that iced the air. She struck him with cold eyes. "No, Thomas, it doesn't *make sense*. It never has! She's a little girl! She doesn't deserve to be this way! She's my baby girl, and she's . . . she's—"

"There's something else." After a deep breath, Thomas explained how his conversation with Robbie had ended the night before. With an eavesdropper.

Mellie paled. "Do they know about Bec?"

"No. They don't seem to. Whoever was listening must not have been there long, because this group came for Robbie. If they knew about Bec . . . they're upset, but they won't find a thing if they're focused on him."

"They won't find a thing? A *mob* is standing outside our home looking for our boy! It doesn't matter that they won't find anything, Thomas. What will they do to him before they figure that out?"

Thomas ground his teeth as he looked through the frosted one-way glass. "Mellie, we know some of these people. They're riled right now, but most of them are just here because they're curious. I told them they can pick two to talk to Robbie with me. I won't be going back out there until everyone else leaves. They're not going to hurt anyone."

"You don't know that."

"I'll protect him! I've protected us before—"

"No, you've *moved* us! We move and we move and we move! The towns get smaller, but the smaller the town, the faster the fingers point at us! When are you going to move us somewhere we can *live?*"

His eyes flared. "You know it's the people that bring this out in her. Living in the city would be a death sentence for everyone around her. There's no hope in the city, no community. We'll find somewh—"

"It isn't working, Thomas! You've tried it and it's just not working. We'll never find a place where she feels completely secure. That doesn't happen! Will you please listen to me? She can get used to people in the city just as well as here. You did! If you really want to protect us, let us leave! These towns are no different than the city." She snarled at the mob on the other side of the pane, a desperate sound that chilled Thomas. "No, they're worse. Everything is magnified here. We can't blend in—we can't hide here!"

"I don't want to hide, Mellie! I've been hiding so much of my life! If we just find the right place, the right people, she won't have to face . . . what I faced. I don't want her to have to run."

"Thomas," her voice softened but remained firm, "you're dreaming. I understand why you're doing this, but it isn't working. She's getting . . . worse. She's getting stronger."

Thomas closed his eyes and leaned his head on the door. Desperation filled him. Stroked him. Whispered seductively, leading him away from his carefully crafted self.

"It's hard, Mellie," he heard himself say, "it's so hard. If I'm going to make this work—teach Bec how to manage—we need to work together. I need to know you're on my side."

"Then we need to be in the city."

Silence consumed him as he considered her ultimatum. The idea of Argon had lured him from the moment he discovered the little town, beckoning to him like a voice from his youth, calling him home. Home, in a country he'd never seen. To think that crossing a border could change their lives was ludicrous, but his fading memory of high school chemistry had helped romanticize the idea: argon, the element that lived on from ancient times to present day; inhaled and expired by billions, from Alexander the Great to Jesus to Shakespeare, down to his own family and those to come; argon, the noble gas that joins the world together. *We are all connected,* he had thought in that moment of weakness. A cornball sentiment that had fooled him with the promise of a better life.

He had forgotten that argon was argon because of its meaning: idle, inert . . . resistant to outside forces and the very idea of change.

He had worked so hard to keep the family curse from devouring his daughter. His years of effort hung like a prized millstone around his neck. He had worked to do what his great-grandfather could not but, like Franz Larsen, he had failed. He could suppress what lurked inside, but he could not defeat it; continuing to try would destroy his family.

"This town doesn't trust us," he admitted, "you're right. We can't stay here anymore."

Mellie's eyes brightened.

"I'm just worried what the city will do to her."

Mellie shook her head, unable to contain her excitement. "I'll work with her every day. We'll help her. I'll do school at home until you agree she's ready. You beat it, Thomas. She will, too. She just needs time. Robbie won't like it, I know, but maybe the fight will change his mind."

Thomas nodded. "We'll stay in a hotel, look for an apartment. We don't have to stay here any longer. We don't have much; we could be gone by the end of the week."

"Why not tonight? We can't send the kids back to school now. Not with the town looking for Robbie. Everything's pretty much suitcase-ready, it's just a matter of packing it."

"I'm not surprised." He managed a defeated smile, then he lowered his voice. "We'll head back south. Should make it easier to cover our trail if anyone decides to track us down. But we'll need to wait till late so nobody sees and calls the border crossing. For now, don't let Bec find out what's happening out there. We don't need any more trouble."

She put a hand on his arm. "I had hoped this would be the place. Really, I did, but—"

"But it's not." Mellie's hand dropped as he turned back to the door. "I know. We'll be gone soon." He glanced outside. "Look at that, Walt actually listened. They're dwindling."

But as Thomas scanned the yard, he saw that the crowd was not shrinking. It was moving. Away from the front door, toward the side of the house.

Toward the cellar.

∞ ∞ ∞

The cellar door caved after Wes Slater's fourth swing of the bat. The rusted padlock had slowed the mob only until Slater spied the Easton maple leaning against the garage. Once the door had split and the padlock was dangling, he stood back to assess his work.

The old hinges creaked as Blackwell yanked the broken panels. He brushed splinters from the frame and peered down into the dark.

"Anybody have a flashlight?"

Within moments, an array of cell phones beamed. Blackwell took the nearest and held it out, illuminating a set of rotting steps. Greenery wound around the knotty planks, descending into darkness. He stepped through the entrance and the wood groaned beneath his heavy feet. Several steps more and he was below ground level. The pit smelled of moss and worms and mould. Several men followed, phones glowing, while Veronica peered down from the splintered hatch.

The air was cool and rank. Blackwell hit bottom and cut a swath across the room with the phone. The area appeared larger than he remembered, consuming the light before it could reach a wall. He saw crates, shelving units, and the edge of a wine rack. He barked at the others for the show of it and they scurried into the darkness, searching.

From where he stood, Blackwell surmised that none of what sat in the cellar belonged to the Larsens. As he suspected. The lock on the now-broken door panels had been the same Master he'd switched out years ago when the last one rusted, and he hadn't really expected Larsen to have found a key. Besides, the family had arrived at the beginning of summer with no fanfare and no moving van. Just a station wagon and a rooftop cargo box. They wouldn't have needed the space—not for what they brought with them, anyway.

He wiped at crates thick with dust and childhood memories. No, this cellar hadn't been disturbed in years.

Of course, Larsen could have dumped the bodies in the river. The divers could have missed them. Or Larsen could have sunk Roseli where the divers had already looked.

But what about the latest boys from school an hour before? The kids blamed Robbie, not his dad. And even if Robbie *had* taken the boys, he couldn't have hidden them with so many other kids around. Blackwell slid a palm through his dusty hair and scratched his scalp.

It didn't make sense. Still, there were too many questions about Larsen that unsettled him. He needed answers, and finding Robbie was the best place to start.

"Walt!" Thomas's frame darkened the small rectangle that opened the world to what lay beneath. "Bring your crew up here!"

Blackwell listened to the men grumble as he made his way to the aged staircase. Slater—unaware that no clue awaited them—whispered, "Stall him. We'll keep looking."

Blackwell reached the foot of the stairs and looked up at the silhouette blocking out the sky. "Apologies for the door, Larsen, but hell, it's mine."

"Anything you find down there has nothing to do with me. Never had the key, as you know. Or your gift for problem-solving."

The older man began a slow climb back to daylight. "You'd be lookin' too, if your kid was missing. You know it."

Thomas stepped aside as Blackwell emerged. "My boy *is* gone, Walt. He hasn't come home from school. Whatever scared the others must have scared him, too. But this is no way to get anywhere. You'll have to let Gilford take it from here."

"You called the cops?" Blackwell was incredulous.

"Mellie doesn't take kindly to intimidation or destruction of property, even if it is yours. She's also not as patient as I am. When your Welcome Wagon crew decided not to leave, she picked up the phone. You don't know her too well, but you're probably lucky she didn't take it up with you herself."

A hint of a smile sparkled in Thomas's eyes, but Blackwell didn't notice. He was staring down the driveway, down the street to where the RCMP cruiser approached. Blackwell shook his head and grinned in disbelief. Response time in Argon was top notch, usually because the boys and girls in blue had nothing else to do.

Then Robbie rolled into view from the opposite direction and started up the driveway on his bike.

"Here he comes!" someone hollered.

Thomas strode toward his son, face pulled tight. Robbie scanned the yard, quizzical eyes bouncing from his dad to the concentration of neighbours milling around the shattered cellar door.

Blackwell kept pace with Thomas a half-step behind. Robbie pulled up and batted his handlebars back and forth nervously between his palms, waiting for someone to speak as the men approached.

Then Wes Slater popped up from the cellar. "The kid's up here!" he shouted down the steps, "Get 'im!"

Blackwell and Thomas were five steps from Robbie when he stomped on his high pedal and bolted. Thomas's arm shot out as he called for his son, but Robbie was already out of reach and gaining speed. Thomas turned to blast Slater, but he and three others were rushing past Thomas out of the yard.

"Git yer cars," Slater shouted as he pursued Robbie around the Park Street bend. The crowd burst like faulty fireworks, running south after Slater and east and west for their cars. Sergeant Gilford shifted from his mosey to a bewildered trot toward Thomas and Blackwell.

"Call them off, Walt!" Thomas growled as he pushed his reddening nose into Blackwell's. Gilford stepped between them and wrestled Thomas back.

Blackwell stumbled away, his face ashen. "I didn't . . . I didn't call them *on!*" An awkward and unfamiliar sense—helplessness?—descended on him as Thomas strained against the sergeant with fury in his eyes. "I can't."

Then Kevin appeared from behind the scuffling men and shouted at Gilford. "Let him go, Nick. Those maniacs are after his son!"

The officer hesitated, then released Thomas. "What's going on?"

Kevin shook his head. "We've got to stop those idiots. They think Robbie's responsible for the missing kids, so Walt led them on this crazy witch hunt!" He looked at Thomas sheepishly. "I'm sorry I didn't stop him, Tom. I didn't know it would . . ." his voice trailed to nothing before changing gears. "He went west, Tom. Any idea where Robbie likes to go?"

Thomas's breath came heavy as he broke his glare at Blackwell. "The river," he said as the first raindrop fell. "He likes to be by the river."

FIFTEEN

The Red River snaked along the western edge of town, bordered by massive pronged cottonwoods. The wooden giants kept watch over Argon, racing from fledgling sprouts to aging sentries in mere decades.

The murmur of the river lapping against its bank dissolved into the fury of a dozen engines roaring as vehicles charged into the treatment plant's gravel parking lot next to the rail bridge. The drivers parked in a circle around the four cars already there like battlefield soldiers surrounding the enemy. The rain fell soft and steady as men and women spilled out into the lot, wielding flashlights like weapons to combat the darkening sky.

Thomas and Kevin stepped out of the police cruiser with Gilford. "Take the trail to Fort Dufferin," Thomas ordered as he pointed at four men, "check everywhere along the way. The rest of us will take the riverbanks. We've got to find him before they do!" He waved a line between the rest of the group and led his crew south, navigating the rocky slope that led to the forest path.

Swelling black clouds blotted out most of the sky. The trees, stretching for heaven and bowing their tips in the wind, blocked what daylight remained.

Three steps into the forest, Blackwell appeared at Thomas's shoulder. "Damn this rain, eh?"

Thomas ignored him.

"You can bet I'll be keeping my slicker in the truck from now on, just in case."

Thomas lowered his head and pressed forward.

"I didn't mean for them to scare him off, Larsen. Slater ain't always thinkin'."

Thomas stopped short and growled. "Don't you blame Slater for this, Walt! You rounded them up! You brought them to my home!" He clutched Blackwell's windbreaker and stabbed at the man with his eyes. "You'd better pray we find him."

Blackwell wrenched free and sidearmed Thomas backward into a small cottonwood. "Don't touch me!" Blackwell snarled. "Man gives an apology and you threaten him?" He glowered at Thomas and straightened his windbreaker. "Larsen, I hope we find your boy. I really do. This town's had enough missing children. But with my granddaughter gone, I won't trust you in this town anymore. You're done. Take the rest of the month, but I won't accept another dollar from you."

Thomas stared at him with unblinking eyes, forehead furrowed. He stepped back onto the path, fists clenched, his breaths ragged and heavy but slowing already, giving way to the years-long habit of calm he had forced upon himself. The calm that he knew was slipping away with every minute that Robbie was missing.

His fight with Blackwell would have to wait. Thomas loosed his fists, then spun and stalked away into the stiffening wind that wasn't yet strong enough to vanquish Blackwell's words.

"But if we find anything—*anything*—that points to you or your boy, I will track you down till the day you die."

∞ ∞ ∞

Beams of light criss-crossed the path and slashed trees as the group roamed together. They had no sky, no guiding star, and soon they would have no path. The group dispersed as those without boots slowed from the thickening paste beneath them.

Thomas called out another reminder to scour the trees since Robbie was a good climber, but he wasn't sure how many could still hear him above the wind. He shone his light up trunks and across branches, ducking the sharp tips that reached for his face. Thomas, tasting rain as he mouthed the words, prayed to catch even a glimpse of his son.

Lightning illuminated the way for brief interludes. Thomas glanced back during one flash and noticed the group straggling, so he shouted his frustration into the wind. "There's not much left to check! Once we hit the clearing by the main bridge, we'll circle back on the outside of the forest. Faster that way."

A multitude of boots slick with mud pressed on. The ground pulled at them now like quicksand, their feet fighting free of the mud with every step. *Shhuck. Shhuck.*

A cry from behind turned Thomas's head. A large branch had broken in the furious wind and knocked Gilford to the ground. Kevin and Veronica freed him from the muck as others gathered. Thomas joined them as Gilford assured everyone he was okay. "Just took a bit of a dusting." Mud glazed his front from tip to toe, wiping him from view between lightning strikes.

"He was lucky, Thomas," Kevin said, "We've got to get out of here soon."

"I'm not leaving till we find Robbie."

"This is getting dangerous."

"I've got to find him, Kevin!"

A blast of lightning lit the forest in white for a lengthy second, revealing Wes Slater and four others fifteen feet ahead on the path, running toward them. They disappeared with the lightning then emerged from the ensuing darkness like shadowy apparitions as they drew closer.

"Where is he, Slater?" Thomas shouted. "Where's Robbie?"

Slater raised both hands in defeat. "Didn't see him! We're heading back. The path's too risky back there."

Blackwell pointed forward. "We're closer to that end, and it's just as bad behind us. No sense turning back now. Once we clear the forest, the ground should get better."

They continued, a dozen strong stumbling through mud and over branches as Thomas led the way. Lightning flashed as they rounded a bend in the path, and a distinct crack sounded over the raging wind. Shouts followed as the group pointed their flashlights in every direction.

"Get back!" someone hollered, as a succession of cracking rippled around them. The group scattered. Seconds later, a large tree tumbled through opposing branches overhead and toppled across the path where some of them had stood a moment before. The tree slammed into the base of an old cottonwood as it landed, snapping one of the thick stalks. The broken prong hung for several seconds, then began to creak. More shouting echoed as everyone scrambled away from the second falling tree. The lumbering cottonwood thundered through the branches of its neighbour, then shook the ground as it crushed the ridge overlooking the shoreline and rolled down the embankment.

The searchers watched the tree roll into the darkness. Blackwell's voice was grim as he broke their silence. "Let's go. We've got to get out of here!"

Thomas watched as the frightened group followed Blackwell along the fallen tree that blocked the path, down the slope toward the riverbank. "What about Robbie? We've got to find him!"

Kevin shouted above the heavy rain and peals of thunder. "We'll keep looking along the way, Tom, but we've got to go!"

Thomas gritted his teeth, watched Kevin turn away, then followed.

SIXTEEN

This was it. The end of their stay in Argon. And it was all Bec's fault.

Robbie hated on his sister all the way through his bike ride after school. He had biked hard and fast around the edge of town, screaming his sister's name in anger for what she had done. She was clueless, yet her response to his plight had sent the students into a panic, and now he couldn't even go home—the adults thought that it was his fault.

His fault. She had tried to help him, but had made things worse. He was certain his parents would tell him they were moving. They couldn't stay after what had happened. Mom would never allow it. Bec had ruined everything. Again.

What bothered Robbie most was not his anger toward Bec, but his fear. Without even thinking, Bec had caused a tree to . . . to come alive. To eat his oppressors.

What would happen when she became angry with *him?*

His heart burned as he wished again that he had been born like his father. Like Bec. He would be able to control it, like his father. He wouldn't have had to run. He wouldn't have let the adults chase him away.

He had ignored the falling rain as he raced from home. He had struggled against the bracing wind gathering force as he reached the riverbank forest. He had burrowed deeper into his hiding place as he heard the storm intensify. And he had decided that he wanted to return home, certain that his pursuers would have given up by now, in these conditions.

Then the ridge where he was hiding collapsed beneath the weight of a tree.

∞ ∞ ∞

Down the slope they marched, led by fear and instinct for survival. The storm rendered their cause forgotten, if only until the trees would not collapse around them under the force of rising wind and angry lightning. Down they marched, over the broken ridge fifteen feet from the river's edge. To their escape route.

They pressed the soft mud with every step, packed the gaps beneath them. Their bodies sank deeper, feet fighting the muddy grasp that threatened to consume them. Rain fell like arrows, pelting their skin, piercing the ground.

Rinsing the path enough for Kevin Grinberg to see the curled hand protruding from the ridge, highlighted by a nasty fork of lightning.

He shouted and shouted until everyone returned. Scores of fingers attacked the ground, casting mud aside, wiping it from the body encased within.

∞ ∞ ∞

Thomas stood at the top of the slope, unable to move as the others surrounded the body. His boy. Robbie.

Robbie.

Robbie!

The storm raged around him in silence as he called his son's name. He stood frozen, held by the same mud that had taken his boy, until he found himself standing suddenly amid the group, lifting Robbie into his arms. His body ached and his heart stopped and his mind screamed in a language as foreign as the chill of death rising from his son's lifeless form.

The sky split and unleashed violent raindrops that could not beat his tears away. He heard nothing but the vibrations of rage and torment rattling his bones, pressing his lungs and throat and nose.

And he wanted everything to disappear.

∞ ∞ ∞

The searchers stood, horrified, as they saw what the tree and their weight had done. Every head turned away as Thomas held his son and wailed.

The river rose from the darkness, welling up around their feet, lapping at their ankles, crashing against the muddy ridge. They forgot Thomas and the dead boy in his arms and ran. The trees clawed them as they stumbled back the way they came, their flashlights swallowed by the dark.

The waves topped the ridge and climbed the slope in pursuit. Gilford slipped and disappeared beneath the surface with hardly a sound. Slater gaped and was taken next. The others abandoned their pride, screaming and shoving as they scrambled to escape.

"Keep moving," Blackwell roared as he pushed his way down the path. The murky water attacked the higher ground in a hyperactive tidal pattern, charging and retreating with the rhythm of an unfocused child. The group fled north as the water broke its west bank, flooding the forest in steady pursuit of its prey.

Kevin followed, casting frequent glances back to gauge the speed of the water. The level rose rapidly, but he was more concerned that more than a minute had passed since he had last seen Thomas, arms wrapped around his son, oblivious. Kevin had pleaded with him to follow, but the man didn't seem to hear.

What would he tell Mellie?

He heard screams ahead and rounded the bend to see his sister on one knee beside a large oak, struggling against the mud at its base.

"The roots have me!" Veronica shouted as he approached. He reached into the mud and seized the hardened vein that slithered into the earth. He tugged, but couldn't brace himself in the thickening sludge. Water crept up as he knelt to use both hands.

Veronica whimpered as the water reached her waist. Kevin fumbled at the root and her boot, his fingers stiffening as the cold water rose. "It's not coming out," he yelled. The water lapped at her neck. She shrieked and stood. "Pull your foot out of the boot. Veronica!" She thrashed, pulling away from the root. "Your foot, not your body, Ronnie. Hurry!"

Kevin plunged his hands back to her boot and tugged at the laces. She flailed, a rigid broken windmill, splashing him as he tried to free her. He tilted his chin up to avoid being submerged and gripped the root to keep from being swept away. He loosened the laces with his free hand and pulled. Her foot moved. "Pull!" he ordered.

She pulled. Her foot sloshed free and she lurched forward with the current. Kevin grabbed at her, but his feet slid in the mud and he fell under. Even submerged, he could hear Veronica's scream. When he surfaced, he heard nothing but the howl of the wind.

"Ronnie!" he shouted. The storm devoured his words and howled back. "Ronnie!" He pushed against the current, stumbling and sliding in the mud, then let the water take him where it had taken his sister. He called her name until he couldn't hear his own voice over the roar of rolling thunder.

Kevin staggered and swam with the current, hoping the water was still pushing landward. He hurtled past bushes and bounced off of trees, trying to minimize the impact by grasping branches to slow his speed. Roots and ruts slapped his feet along the way, threatening to catch and pull him under.

Then the water spit him from the forest, casting him up the embankment that led to the parking lot. He looked for Veronica on the slope and down toward the river and saw nothing.

She was gone.

Water ran up the slope, covering his ankles. Kevin gathered himself and climbed the embankment. The cruiser and several other vehicles remained at the top, but he saw no one but Terry, waiting.

"Have you seen Ronnie? We got separated!"

Kevin staggered to his brother-in-law, dripping river and tears. "She's gone, Terry. The water took her."

Terry's face sunk. "What? No!"

"It's still coming, Terry. It's not far behi—"

"Did you see her, man? How do you know?"

"I tried to help her, Terry, I'm sorry. I'm so sorry I couldn't help her!"

"No!" Terry struck Kevin suddenly with both hands, sending him tumbling into shallow water that hadn't been there a moment before. "She can't be dead, too!"

"Terry—"

"She can't be! Help me find her!"

"It's *coming,* Terry!"

"We have to find her!" He crumpled to the rocky earth and covered his face with his hands. "We have to find Jimmy!"

Kevin thought of Roseli again and wept. He stood and offered Terry his hand as death crept up around them. "We have to go, Terry." The man didn't budge, so Kevin shook Terry's shoulders. "We stay here, we'll die."

Terry batted him away, stood, and began walking down the slope. Into the water.

"Dammit, Terry!" Kevin ran down and wrapped an arm around his brother-in-law's chest, and dragged him back six feet before the element of surprise wore off. Then Terry found his footing and resisted. He spun and swung upward, connecting a hard left to the side of Kevin's head. Kevin collapsed into three inches of water and hit the gravel hard.

Terry turned and walked on.

Stunned and prone, Kevin turned his head slowly, scraping his nose and cheek against gravel in time to see Terry wade back into the water and rush down the slope, out of sight. He wanted to scream out at Terry as he had for Ronnie, but only found energy enough to watch the swirling waves through the stars dancing numbly in his head.

The water rose again and he choked as it slithered through his nose and mouth. He lifted his head and coughed it out in gasps that became moans, pathetic and mournful, as he thought of his nephew, his daughter, his sister, and now his brother-in-law.

Taken by the water, the wind, and God knew what else. Just gone.

The waves lapped higher, licking his cheeks and nose once more.

He thought of Susanna and Trent—still alive and waiting—and

willed himself onto all fours, then spat out mud from his lips and tongue and stood. Mist sprayed his face between the tears as the water inched higher. Mourning his lost would have to wait.

Kevin entered the cruiser and turned the key with mud-black fingers, gazing back at the raging menace. If it kept its pace, the dike would breach in minutes.

He had to warn everyone.

SEVENTEEN

Mellie glanced at the faint green sky for the umpteenth time since Kevin had raced through the neighbourhood, bellowing from a police cruiser bullhorn about an impending dike breach. The storm clouds continued to march closer, though when she ran up their back yard dike to check the water level, the river hadn't risen an inch. Nonetheless, the engines revving along the block were enough for her. Something was happening.

She heaved her son's suitcase into the station wagon and steadied the pile of boxes and bags. She hadn't had time to pack neatly, but their clothes and irreplaceables were ready. Now if only Thomas and Robbie would come back, they could all leave.

And they could just keep driving and escape this town without suspicion. The storm threatening their homes would provide perfect cover.

Bec huffed as she dragged a garbage bag of toys and stuffed animals to the car. Mellie had tried to keep her busy to keep her mind off the stream of frantic neighbours abandoning Park Street and, in all likelihood, Argon. Frightening Bec would only lead to disaster.

Bec left the bag for her mother and climbed into the middle seat.

Mellie fought the urge to drive around town to search for her boys. She knew that Thomas would bring Robbie home as soon as he found him, and it wouldn't help to be out driving when they returned. But the storm was drawing closer. If the dike behind them *did* breach, she would have little time to react. She would have to leave their home soon, boys or no.

The police cruiser! The thought stopped her hand in mid-swing on the wagon's back door. Kevin had driven by in the police cruiser, the same car that Thomas had taken to reach the river. How could they come home quickly without their ride?

She ran to the driver's seat, launched a herky-jerky three-point turn, and aimed for the end of the long driveway.

∞ ∞ ∞

"No more. We're leaving." Kevin threw another duffel into the back of his Jeep and motioned for his family to get in.

He decided they would exit at the northeast route on Willems Road. That would mean a long detour back to the main highway, but Willems Road was closer to home and he didn't want to risk the southwest bridge being flooded out. If they found out the hard way, they might not have enough time to double back.

But they couldn't leave yet. Kevin couldn't ignore the deep sadness that had gnawed at him since he passed the Larsen's yard on his way home. Now that his wife and son were ready to go, he knew what he had to do.

He had to talk to Mellie Larsen.

∞ ∞ ∞

ARGON

The sturdy old station wagon had rumbled only halfway down the driveway when the figure appeared in the distance. The edge of the storm had reached the estate and the rain pelted harder, blurring the windshield despite the rapid sing-song rhythm of the wipers. Mellie saw the silhouette and her heart raced.

She pressed the pedal and closed the distance between them in seconds. The headlights struck the figure, and Thomas emerged from the darkness, Robbie's limp form draped over his arms.

Mellie froze.

No!

She stared at her son's mud-streaked face, clumped hair, slick clothing. A wet lump of clay that had lost the breath of God.

She stared at her husband's stony face, blood red eyes, broken spirit. A sopping mass of pain and despair.

They hurtled closer. She yanked the steering wheel sharply, fish-tailing off the driveway as she floored the brake pedal. She opened the car door and Bec peered out from the back seat. "Robbie!"

Mellie raced around the front of the car and wrapped her arms around Robbie's body, moaning. The trees lining the driveway began to groan as the wind gripped them.

"They crushed him, Mellie!"

"No! No!" She shook with huge, rasping sobs. She pressed her face against Robbie's muddy cheek and cried. Sleet beat down on them. "What . . . what happened? No!"

"The riverbank."

"What?" Hail attacked the station wagon in staccato bursts. Mellie flinched against the icy stones and looked through the enormous storm to see overflowing ditches. She looked back to the house with saucer eyes and saw a thin film of river sliding over the peak and down the dike toward them. "Is that you? Are you doing this?"

Thomas closed his eyes. "I'm so tired."

Mellie's legs quivered. She needed to sit, to fold. She needed Thomas to hold her so she could collapse. "You have to stop! If you can't stop this, we have to go, Thomas! We have to leave now!"

She pulled him toward the passenger seat. He clung to Robbie as she tucked them in and closed the door. She cried out as a plum-sized hailstone drilled her shoulder while she circled the car. Once inside, she adjusted the gear and stomped the accelerator.

Bec looked at Robbie and wailed from the back seat. A funnel spawned from the center of the largest storm cloud. She sobbed, and the center of the funnel caved inward, forming a small porthole as the car raced alongside the giant cloud.

Mellie felt the colour drain from her face down to her soles. *The funnel was fashioning a mouth.*

Bec cried harder and the mouth grew. The cone breached the edge of the estate as it drew closer to the beat-up wagon, clipping the towering pines and sending treetops spinning into the air. Mellie pulled her eyes from the sight and sped south, narrowly missing Kevin's Jeep rushing toward them. Kevin and Susanna gaped at the menacing tornado and veered from its path. Mellie couldn't be sure from the rearview mirror, but the Jeep appeared to dodge the funnel before the dark cloud cut off her sight line.

The cloud appeared to be growing exponentially, blotting out entire blocks of homes behind them as the station wagon screamed through Argon's asphalt grid. Telephone wires and poles snapped as the storm bore down on the Caprice, and Mellie tried to shake the hideous sense that the funnel was following them. It was impossible, but the storm had come from the west with Thomas and had turned (or *grown*) south in sync with when they drove away.

Shingles, siding, and lawn ornaments twirled in the air like ash from a campfire. Trees bowed and broke around them, while the leaves two blocks ahead hung limply, yet untouched by the looming edge of the storm. Debris vanished into the mouth of the vortex like flies into the night. Thomas clutched Robbie with his eyes sealed, head down, body trembling.

The funnel brushed the town hall, spewing century-old bricks in all directions. Brick and hail pounded the roof of the car. Staggering cracks networked across the windshield like an ice floe imploding. Bec huddled in the back seat, screaming.

The storm filled the rearview mirror as Mellie weaved southwest through the wet streets toward the river, toward the green bridge, praying aloud that it would still be standing. Water crashed up from the ditches against the sides of the vehicle and the road disappeared, leaving no path but her memory. The thin sheet of water around them had become a roiling carpet.

Mellie tightened her grip on the wheel until her fingers were nearly translucent.

Thomas rolled his head and spoke, hardly audible above the roar around them. "Faster."

There was no faster. The pedal was on the floor but the water kept them from putting the storm out of reach. "How can we get away?" she yelled. "It's her! She's doing this! We can't get away from *her!*"

Houses imploded and the town hospital crumbled as the storm blazed down Main Street. Through momentary lapses in the dark cloud, Mellie glimpsed swaths of the riverside forest burning, sweeping westward over the dike toward Main. Sections of chain link fencing danced beside them as they passed the baseball diamond. Two blocks to the main road. Less than a minute to the bridge.

The thick water slapped like mud against the wheels.

Mellie navigated the final right turn and straightened the wheel.

To her right, something exploded and Mellie realized that they were passing Walt's Wrench & Gas (or just Walt's Wrench now, if the Gas had detonated inside the hungry cloud). She hardly had time to wonder whether Walt had been inside, but the image struck her of a defiant Blackwell standing outside his shop with the bay door up, shaking his wrench at the oncoming storm.

The funnel was now seconds behind. Ahead, beyond the river and its fiery banks, the silent sky faded to grey. Between the car and the bridge, however, five hundred yards of storm nipped at the edge of the road, threatening to block them completely. Mellie shut out her daughter's wails and her son's stillness and flattened the pedal once more.

The back end of the station wagon undulated as the rising water ripped the tires from the pavement. The tires caught again long enough for the car to shoot forward like a brown and beige bullet. Dark clouds enveloped the vehicle and Mellie whimpered loudly. She was blind, guided only by the sound of the funnel behind them. She held the steering wheel as straight as she could manage, aiming for the middle of the bridge based on her last line of sight.

She heard the muffled but familiar crepitation of the bridge's crisscross pattern beneath the tires and shouted a prayer of thanks that they hadn't hit either railing post head-on. Then the sound of tires on metal was gone, swept away by the thickening water as it sent them spinning. The car swerved and slammed its rear corner against the side of the bridge, then careened off toward the opposite rail. Mellie's mental compass floundered as the water tossed them like rags in the spin cycle. She clasped the wheel not for steering control but to keep from being thrown against her window, and heard the faux wood panel crumple as the Caprice collided with the railing. Thomas, oblivious to all but Robbie in his arms, fell across the bench seat and

ARGON

pinned Mellie to the door. She gasped and pushed against him, but fell back as the wind shoved the wagon back against the railing then lifted the passenger side wheels, tilting the car into the side of the bridge. Mellie screamed as the wheels slammed back down and bounced, tipping the wagon back against the rails. *It's trying to kill us,* she thought as her husband tumbled into her again. *The wind or the water or* something *is trying to kill us.*

The bridge groaned like an old man giving way to gravity. Whether the sound began at the railing or the roadway Mellie could not tell; for all she knew, the sound was borne of the storm itself. The groans continued, increasing in volume and vibrato until they consumed even the overbearing whine of the funnel itself. The wagon's rear dipped suddenly as the bridge buckled beneath it, and in a momentary vision Mellie attributed to the clarity of one's final breath, she saw the '88 Chevy Caprice from overhead (gleaming like the day it rolled off the assembly line, of course; if she had to die in a quarter-century old clunker, it was at least going to *look* brand new), sliding backward and toppling end over end as the bridge gave way. They fell, the four of them, into the rushing Red River as the storm screamed around them all the way down.

Then the vision was gone and Mellie jammed her foot down in desperation. The tachometer jumped to red. The wheels touched down through the rising water—water that should have drained through the bridge's grid pattern floor—and the car lurched forward, kicking water up as Mellie straightened the wagon and sped away. They broke through the darkest clouds and she saw land ahead. And pavement! She felt the *thump-thump* transition from metal bridge to wet highway shiver through her knees. The water shrank back and she noticed that although the funnel was still large in her rearview mirror, it looked suddenly smaller. The storm clouds faded even as they continued their pursuit, shrinking and slowing until the mouth of the funnel, then the tornado itself, disappeared.

Mellie kept driving, refusing to stop until fatigue and anguish consumed her.

EIGHTEEN

Mellie stood at the edge of the road, watching her husband cradle their dead son in his lap. He had laid Robbie's body on the roof of the car during the night, while she dreamed of frightening creatures whisking Bec away.

Dawn was breaking on the far side of Argon, adding an ominous glow to the smoldering town.

"Why do you suppose it stopped?"

Thomas sat, rigid, eyes closed. "I think she blacked out. The pressure must have been intense, in her head. I . . . just remember that she stopped wailing."

"But it wasn't just her."

"No."

Mellie turned away.

"Can you control it again?"

She didn't want the truth, but she had nothing else to say. She felt so far from Thomas, wishing she could stop the sickness growing between them. His anger had spawned much more devastation than Argon would ever see: mistrust. She had only seen him lose control once before—a long time ago—but it had been nothing like this. Their son was dead. What if Thomas couldn't suppress his grief? Couldn't find himself again?

"I don't know . . . if I want to."

Mellie drew Bec close as the sun inched higher. If Thomas gave up, Bec would be lost. She needed a guide to help her navigate this cruelty. Mellie crumbled inside at the awful thought: she could never give her daughter what she needed most.

Bec needed her father.

Thomas stared from atop the station wagon, watching smoke weave across the eastern sky. The fields quieted around them, leaving the faint crackle of flame singing in the distance.

"We need to go back."

Mellie's mouth fell open.

"I'm going to bury him. This is where he wanted to be."

Mellie clutched her daughter, squeezed her tighter as tears splashed the young golden locks. She couldn't go back. She hated the town for killing Robbie. She hated them all for killing the Thomas she knew.

"And there might be survivors. We have to help them."

Mellie buried her face in Bec's hair and sobbed. There was that. The one seed of comfort in her season of agony: she loved his heart.

It was why they still had hope.

∞ ∞ ∞ ∞ ∞

Coming soon!

Thomas Larsen vanishes from a hospital hallway and appears in a deadly world where terrifying creatures threaten at every turn. During a desperate search for his wife and daughter, he must navigate the ashes of this desolate world where the shadows themselves can't be trusted, and escape the clutches of a crazed man with secrets as dangerous as his own.

When Thomas discovers the truth of why his family disappeared, the revelation thrusts him into an unthinkable future from which he may never return.

Available soon at ELPatrick.com and your favourite bookstores!

Read on for an excerpt

About the Author

E. L. Patrick is a fourth-generation Canadian whose ancestral origin is steeped in mystery. He writes about people restored and devastated by choices, and about who we are behind the masks.

He lives in the heart of North America, in the majestic sprawl of God's prairie, with his wife and children.

www.ELPatrick.com

∞ ∞ ∞

Share your support with an honest review
on your favourite book retailer's site.

Acknowledgments

Lisa, for your love, support, and the time to wander in my worlds.

My early readers: Tyson, Adam, Rhéal, David, and Steve. Thanks for your time and useful feedback!

The character name Kevin Grinberg is a tuckerization, fulfilling a years-ago promise when Gmail was but a gleam in Google's eye. Thanks for the account invitation way back when, Kevin!

Dean Wesley Smith, for sharing what you know.

This story started as a brief "Write Off" entry on my website that wouldn't go away. Thanks to my readers and subscribers for your encouragement in the opening days of Argon's life.

∞ ∞ ∞

THE
REAPPEARING
MAN

E. L. PATRICK

Excerpt from

THE REAPPEARING MAN

The masked men emerged from silent shadows and surrounded the rusting beige station wagon. From his place behind the wheel, Thomas made out four shapes walking. The others would soon surprise him.

The night was black with occasional punctures of moonlight. Clouds drifted across the moon like heavenly sailors tossed about in a slow-motion sea storm.

Thomas grabbed the key from the dash and twisted it in the ignition. The four shapes froze for a singular moment as the engine roared and the headlamps blasted the night away around them; then they bolted for the doors. Thomas cranked the gearshift and hit the pedal. The wagon lurched between the pairs of black-clad attackers, jolting Mellie and Bec awake as it sped down the strip of farm road where Thomas had parked for the night.

"What's happening?" Mellie called from the middle seats, her voice tight. Bec had sat up from her mother's lap and was curled in the nook of Mellie's arm, rubbing her eyes with a small fist.

"We're leaving." He recounted what he had seen, thankful for the first time that his sleep had been slipping away since leaving Argon.

The roof dimpled and popped like the safety seal on the lid of a Bernardin, starting at the rear and working toward the windshield. Someone was above them. Thomas jerked the steering wheel back and forth to try to shake off the stowaway. Bec began crying.

The dimples stopped above the driver's seat. A moment later, Thomas's window shattered and a hand reached in and grabbed him by the hair. He shouted and grabbed at the roof rider with his left hand while trying to keep sight of the road by the two swaths of headlight. The attacker pulled and Thomas resisted, fighting the pain even as he imagined the hand breaking free with a clump of hair and scalp.

The Caprice dipped as the driver's side left the road and found grass. The roofer's legs slid over the edge and his grip tightened on Thomas's hair. Thomas ground his teeth together and bellowed. He could feel the twinge in his head that he had spent so many years learning to suppress. It entered like a harmless thought, but he knew what inevitable spiral nipped at its heels. Thomas's long-held desire to spurn the sensation had died with his son in Argon, and he had come to embrace this harbinger.

The feeling started numbly, then swept through his head like overwhelming prickles of paresthesia, that tingling of limbs and nerves waking from their slumber.

The sense had toppled him the first few times he'd entertained it after Robbie's death, brought on by unexpected bouts of rage or depression. Thomas took to the nearest fields for solace and lived out of the station wagon with Mellie and Bec awhile, attempting to quell the anger seeping through him, attempting to regain control. If not for himself, for Bec.

If the demolition of Argon was any indication, he suspected Bec's version of the ability was more powerful than his own, and hers was only beginning to develop. How could he protect his daughter from herself if *he* didn't have the will to fight?

He had made progress in recent weeks, Mellie told him, though he didn't feel that way. Each time he remembered holding Robbie's lifeless body or dropping the first shovelful of dirt on him, he wanted to let go and let the beast within take over.

It *was* a beast. He knew it by the way it tracked him down and held him in its grip. That wasn't progress, not freedom. The only freedom he had came after he surrendered himself to this thing and was rid of it again.

Until the next time.

Bec was screaming. Mellie clawed at the roof rider's hand from behind the head rest, trying to pry it free of Thomas's hair. Thomas managed to keep one hand on the wheel while struggling to keep his eyes forward. The old wagon jostled along erratically as his foot slipped from the accelerator to the brake and back again.

A tree branch whipped at the windshield and snagged the roofer. The man screamed as he was pulled—*taken*—from the top of the car, and Thomas echoed the sound as the man took a piece of his scalp through the window frame. Thomas's vision went blood red. The world flew by in a passionate scream. Thomas couldn't see anything around him; he only *sensed* it. He could distinguish the brightness of the headlights, barely—the night was red death, the light was pinkish—but couldn't see where the car was going. The Caprice trembled with each rut and rock that rolled under the tires. Perhaps the old wagon always did that, but without sight to distract him, Thomas felt the car's shiver in every bone. He gripped the wheel tighter and saw two strips of pinkish dots poke through the red where his knuckles should have been. Then he felt everything tip left—the car had abandoned the road completely—and jerked his head right to avoid bashing the jagged remains of the driver's window.

Thomas stomped the floor and caught the edge of one of the pedals. The engine revved. He stomped again, further left, and the car groaned as the brakes engaged. The station wagon settled on a tilt, slamming Thomas against the driver door. He still saw red, though black bled in slowly from the edges.

"Mellie!" he called. "Stay in the car!"

He fumbled for the door latch and gripped the frame to keep from falling as he opened the door. He stepped out and ended up in a drunken crouch as he navigated the incline of the ditch. He made his way down to the flattest ground as more of the dark night dripped into view. Thomas couldn't see where the roofer had landed, but if a tree had gotten him, he would be trouble no more.

The red dissolved into the colourless void of dim moonlight, and soon Thomas could make out shapes around him; the car on the embankment to his left, its blank eyes staring down the road behind him; the row of large trees to his right, guarding the field beyond the ditch, their branch tips intertwined like fingers clasping.

Six figures approached, running hard, lit by the bare streak of moonlight breaking through the trees. The roofer's friends had closed the gap and were almost at the station wagon. Almost to Mellie and Bec.

Thomas shouted from the bottom of the ditch, hoping to distract them. It worked, mostly. Four of the runners changed course and charged down toward him. Thomas braced himself, waited until they were nearly on him, then threw himself at their shins, stretching himself into a human tripwire. Three of them tumbled over him and Thomas felt two boots sharply in his ribs and thigh. The fourth two-stepped over Thomas's sprawling form and jumped on him before the sting had softened.

"Get the needle!" he shouted as he dug a knee in Thomas's back.

Thomas struggled against his attacker, who clearly had pounds on his side. Another presence—dark and heavy—dropped down beside him. Thomas thrashed harder as he envisioned the needle, long and hungry, poised to plunge.

Then he heard Mellie's and Bec's screams. Even with his head pressed to the ground, he could see dimly a tangle of feet atop the ditch as the other agents pulled his wife and daughter from the car.

He shouted Mellie's name and the ground came alive. Tendrils of tree root burst through the soil around him like depth charges exploding. The ground shifted beneath them and Thomas sunk a little. Dirt splattered his eyes and nose as a root shot up inches from his face. He saw a flash of light from the top of the ditch and heard screams from the men and Bec, but not Mellie.

Not Mellie.

Wind whipped his face and mixed with the screams in his ears, and all he knew—all he could hear—was that Mellie wasn't screaming anymore.

Someone yelled to "get the girl!" The weight on Thomas vanished as something lifted his attacker, but the ground began shifting as he scrambled up so he couldn't find a foothold. He was sinking; the earth was suddenly soft and loose and swallowing him. *Was this Bec's doing or his own?*

Branches swiped at the remaining attackers, flailing as though a fierce wind storm had settled on the nearest three trees while their neighbours stood still. Thomas stretched his arms high as he slid lower in the soil, and his fingers found a branch as it swung above him. The branch's momentum tugged him free of the dirt with a *pop* and he clung to the knotty life preserver as it carried him to safety.

From the air, Thomas watched with wide eyes as roots wrapped around the head and shoulders of the last attacker and drew him into the earth. The man's screams rang sharply but were muffled quickly as his head entered the soil, leaving silent, kicking legs until those, too, were drawn underground.

Thomas clung to the branch and watched the remaining roots slither back beneath the surface. When the earth stopped moving, Thomas dropped to the ground and raced toward the small, crumpled form near the station wagon. He swallowed against the lump that cracked in his dry throat like eggshell.

"Mellie!" he shouted into the night, "Mellie, where are you?"

He reached his daughter's body and saw the glister on her face even before he knelt to cradle her in his arms. Blood, looking black under the clouded sky. The flesh was torn along Bec's chest and neck and her face below the nose, leaving her eyes and brow untouched as though she had tied a terrible bandanna round her mouth in a dust storm. One of the trees had struck her in its moment of rage—in *his* moment of rage. While trying to protect her.

His breath stopped. Grief poured from him in great guttural sobs as he clutched Bec to his chest. He called her name and Mellie's over and over with wild, hopeless screams.

But no one answered.

sign up for notifications at ELPatrick.com

THE REAPPEARING MAN